and the Fisher-Cat

By Virginia Voight

First published in 1953

This unabridged version has updated grammar and spelling.

© 2018 Jenny Phillips

Cover illustration by Kessler Garrity

Table of Contents

ALGONQUIN WORDS. 1

1. A NEWFANGLED GUN 2

2. INTO THE WILDERNESS. 11

3. NEMOX 21

4. FAIR TRADE. 27

5. THE RENFIELD POCCONOCK. 34

6. TROUT FOR BREAKFAST 42

7. PET PANTHER. 52

8. MOVE AWAY!. 60

9. RAID 67

10. UNCAS 76

11. WATCH THE RED BELT! 83

12. PEQUOT COUNTRY 91

13. ONE AGAINST MANY 98

14. YELLOW JACKETS 103

15. THE BIG BOULDER 111

16. HOBOMOKO SPEAKS 120

17. DOWN THE RIVER 127

18. FLAMING ARROWS. 133

19. UPSTREAM 140

Algonquin Words

Hijah: Goodbye

Hobomoko: Thunder God

Koue: Greetings, Friend!

Loks: Panther

Matchit-Moodus: Place of Noises. Moodus cave is in East Haddam, Connecticut. Geologists believe that the noises and tremors are traceable to faulting in the underlying rock.

Mohegan: Wolf

Nemox: Fisher; Fisher-cat; Martes pennanti

Netops: Goodbye

Owanux: English

Pequot: Destroyer

Pequot River: Now called Thames

Pocconock: Natural Meadow

Pyquog: Dancing Place

Upweekis: Lynx

Wah: No

CHAPTER 1

A Newfangled Gun

Zeke Renfield ran his fingers through his thatch of sandy hair as he stood looking at the heap of stuff in the middle of the woodshed floor. It all had to be sorted and ready to load for leaving Plymouth the next morning.

For days he had been going over it, trying to cull out every single thing that his uncle, cousin, and he could possibly do without when they got to the frontier. They would have only one packhorse and so Zeke had to plan the load carefully. But for every article he had cast aside, his uncle or cousin seemed to have added two of something else.

He removed a heavy sack of books from the heap for the third or fourth time and shook his head as he looked at his list of items that had to be loaded somehow. Iron pans, brass kettle, roll of quilts and sheets, the ax, the plow, the precious seeds that would give them their first crop in the new land. All these were sheer necessities. Bullet molds, bars of lead, a keg of powder—

He pulled out a sack that had been artfully hidden under some other things. Angrily he ripped off the cord to peer inside. A froth of pink ostrich plumes puffed into his face, tickling his nose.

Judith's fine London hat. Of all the silly things! What would she want with a hat like this out on a new homestead in the wilds of Connecticut?

"Zeke!" Judith darted at him from the doorway and snatched the hat away.

Zeke gritted his teeth. "I ought to toss it into the Bay! I told you yesterday there's no room on our load for useless stuff."

"My father says I may take it!" Over the plumes her green eyes shot sparks at him.

She seemed like a round little kitten, all bristled up and ready to fight.

Judith was eleven years old. Old enough, Zeke had heard his mother tell her, to be a real help to him and her father when they reached the frontier. So far, though, she didn't seem to understand just how rugged the life out there would be.

"You only get to take one sack of clothes," he reminded her flatly. "Those plumes won't keep you warm next winter when you're howling for a woolen petticoat."

"I'll thank you to let me do my own choosing!"

Zeke swung abruptly back to his packing.

Judith flounced toward the door. Before she reached it her father came into the shed.

Nobody ever looked less like a pioneer than scholarly Master George Renfield with his peaked, silver mustache and beard. It was only a month since he had arrived from England with his motherless daughter, to try his fortune in the New World. Now he was going out as a schoolmaster to the new settlement of Wethersfield.

He glanced from the pile of luggage to the sack of books which had been dragged aside. "Did you remove my books again, Ezekiel?"

"Yes, sir. There's no room for books."

"Nonsense. The books must go. I need them for my work in school."

"There will be no bread in Connecticut except what we provide for ourselves," Zeke explained. "Farm tools and seeds are the important things. Books will come later."

"Do you not think I am the one to decide which things are most important to us?"

"No, sir."

Master Renfield's eyes flashed at that.

Zeke realized with a pang that Uncle George thought he was being undutiful.

"Uncle George, I'm the one who has to see that we get enough to eat," he said earnestly.

His uncle gave him a long look. Then he picked up the sack of books and left the shed.

He tore into the pile of luggage again, heaving things this way and that. Girls' gewgaws! Old men's books! It was a good thing there was one practical member of the family.

"Zeke," said a small voice. It was Judith, still clutching the plumed hat. "My father wouldn't know what to do without books. Maybe I can leave out some clothes to make room for them."

"No!" Zeke threw the word over his shoulder.

"You needn't be so cross." Judith sounded hurt.

Zeke swung around to face her. "I'm not cross, Judy, but you and Uncle George just don't understand. You're going to need your clothes. It will be a long time before you'll get any more. Books we won't need."

Judith looked at him with fear and went slowly into the house.

He kept telling himself he had the right of it. Yet how could his uncle open the school and teach without books?

Not that Zeke cared whether school was kept or not, but without the school they probably would not be going to Connecticut at all.

He threw down what he was doing and tramped impatiently into the house.

The big kitchen was filled with the glow and cheerful bustle of suppertime. Zeke's mother and Hope, his sister, were settling the table boards on trestles. Judith, on a stool by the fireplace, was supposed to be turning the roast upon the spit. Instead she was teasing the kitten with a bit of ribbon.

The smell of burning meat brought Goodwife Renfield rushing to the fireplace. "Judith! The roast!" she chided gently.

With a sigh Judith took hold of the spit handle.

Zeke sniffed the scorched meat anxiously as he crossed the room. Judith would be doing the cooking in Connecticut. What kind of meals would she give them?

Master Renfield sat reading by the light of a bayberry candle.

"Uncle George."

"What's that?" Master Renfield looked up absently. It took him a moment to pull his thoughts off the printed page and recognize his nephew. "Oh, it's you, Ezekiel."

"Yes, sir. Uh—Uncle George, I think I can make room for some of your books in the load."

Master Renfield glanced across the room to Zeke's father who said quietly, "We were hoping that you might manage to, Zeke."

"I've been thinking books are important too." Zeke paused, and then his clear gray eyes met his uncle's gaze squarely. "But not as important as food will be at the first."

His uncle closed his book and stood up. "I like a boy who has the courage to stand by his own convictions and yet can have a thought for the needs and beliefs of other people." He looked at Zeke's father again and nodded. Then he walked slowly to his own room.

Alan and Roger, Zeke's older brothers, came into the kitchen. "Well, Zeke," said Alan, "by this time tomorrow you will be well out along the wilderness trail."

Zeke felt a twinge at the thought of how much he'd miss them. "I wish you were all going with us."

"We'll be along next year," his father reminded him.

The arrival of many new colonists at Plymouth had made living conditions too crowded there. When explorers brought reports of the wonderfully rich soil and the abundance of fur in the Connecticut Valley, many people began to talk of moving west and founding new colonies. Goodman Renfield was one of these. He had decided to move to the frontier settlement of Wethersfield. The family could not leave yet because he had almost a year's work to finish, as a cabinetmaker here in Plymouth. But his brother, who had just come from England, accepted the position of schoolmaster there and so had to go at once.

The two older boys, Alan and Roger, were needed too much by the family here to be spared; so Zeke and his uncle were to be the advance scouts for the family. They would buy land from the Indians and establish a homestead.

Zeke was fourteen, only two years younger than Plymouth Colony itself. He had grown up with the Colony. Knowledge of hunting, gardening, and all the other things that a homesteader must know, had come to him naturally. He was a good shot too and self-reliant in the woods. Tall and rangy with broad shoulders and big competent hands, Zeke looked to be of the stuff of which good pioneers are made.

Master Renfield came out of his room and joined his brother and nephews. The three boys, as well as their father, looked eagerly at the long-barreled musket he was carrying.

It was a handsome piece with a stock of fine grained beech wood, beautifully inlaid with silver. More than this, it was a flintlock musket of the most modern French make. Before the arrival of Master Renfield of England, the only person in Plymouth to own such a firearm had been Captain Myles Standish. The other Pilgrims still used slow-burning matchlock guns.

Until now Uncle George had kept the marvelous gun in his own room. None of the boys had had a chance to examine it, but they had discussed it often among themselves. Now Zeke sighed inwardly as he glanced from the slim, efficient looking musket to the cumbersome old blunderbuss on the wall, which his father had given him to use in Connecticut.

Uncle George walked over to him and laid the musket in his hands. "This gun is for you, Ezekiel. With it you will shoot meat for our table and defend us from the red savages, if need be, which God forbid."

Zeke's fists closed hard upon the flintlock. In his wildest dreams he had never expected to own a gun like this. He could scarcely believe this blessing. But when he tried to tell his uncle how he felt about it the right words would not come. "Zooks, Uncle George! I—I don't know how to thank you."

"Then do not try. You are welcome to the gun. "

Zeke's father and brothers clustered around, eager for a closer look at the musket. Two of its features interested them especially. One was the "sight," an ingenious newfangled device mounted on the barrel. The other was the amazing new flintlock method of firing the powder. Zeke had handled Captain Standish's gun and knew the value of these improvements. A trained marksman was almost certain to hit what he aimed at with a flintlock, which was by no means true with the old-fashioned matchlocks.

Goodman Renfield looked the musket over carefully, and then handed it to Alan and Roger. The brothers exclaimed over it as they took turns sighting along the barrel.

Zeke's heart swelled with pride as he watched them.

"It's too fine a weapon for a young cub," said Roger.

Alan laughed. "Zeke's a better shot than either of us."

Zeke took the musket back and cradled it lovingly in his arm.

He went closer to the candle, so that he might better examine the intricate mechanism of the lock. When his mother called them to supper he took his gun with him and leaned it against the bench, where he sat between Hope and Judith. His hand kept straying out to pat the barrel.

It gave him a feeling of new confidence to know that on the morrow, when he set out into unknown country, this gun would be going with him. Already he felt as though it were a part of him. In Connecticut he would never let it be more than a hand's reach away from him.

CHAPTER 2
Into the Wilderness

Zeke rolled out of his bed in the attic with the first glimmer of dawn the next day. The morning star, glittering like a frost crystal in the pale bit of sky framed by his little window, told him that it was going to be a fair day.

Hurry made his hands all thumbs as he pulled on his new breeches and jerkin of hickory-dyed homespun and tied the points that fastened his green woolen hose to his breeches at the knee.

A delicious feeling of freedom surged all through him as he started toward the ladder-like stairs that led down to the kitchen. Out there on the frontier, with only his absent-minded old Uncle George in authority, he'd be practically his own master!

His mother was busy about the kitchen fireplace. Zeke's excitement ebbed when he saw her. He began already to feel homesick. What would life be like far from her and father?

She hugged him. "Sit down, Son. I'll give you breakfast. Father and the boys are feeding the stock and making up the pack for you."

She had cooked all the things that he liked best. Cornmeal

mush with cream and maple sugar, and golden flecks of butter floating on the cream. An omelet so light that it was a wonder it did not float away. Hot muffins with dried blueberries speckling their melting goodness.

"I'll dream of these muffins in Connecticut," Zeke said, buttering his third. "Judy is not much of a cook."

"You must be patient while she learns," his mother answered. "She's been used to having servants to do all the things that we know how to do for ourselves. But she tries hard. I am sure she will make out."

Zeke managed to fit several of his uncle's books into the luggage, but Judith's hat had been sternly ruled out. However, when she came out of the house, she was dressed for the trail in a russet gown, long cape, buckled shoes, and the hat! With its froth of curly pink plumes it was perched at a saucy angle on her hair.

"It's the prettiest hat I ever had," she explained to Zeke's look of astonishment. "I just can't leave it behind."

Zeke reached out and tweaked one of her chestnut curls. "Don't blame me then if some Indian tries to tomahawk you to get those plumes for his scalp lock."

Her eyes widened with fear of the unknown wilderness. The kitten came purring against her petticoat. She picked him up and hugged him tight, as if she were glad to hold on to something dear and familiar. "Oh, Tabby Paws! I wish I could take you along for company."

"Faugh! You'll have Marigold. A cow's as good as a kitten any day." Zeke handed Judith a willow switch he had cut that morning. "It will be your task to keep Marigold on the trail. Whack her with this if she tries to stray."

Judith looked uneasy as she took the switch. Her aunt had taught her to milk, but a cow still seemed a large, frightening animal to her.

"Here comes Master Elkins!" Zeke called to his uncle as a merry jingle of harness bells rang on the air.

A string of packhorses came plodding along the road. Ahead of them strode Bejoyful Elkins, the Wethersfield trader. The people there had commissioned him to find them a schoolmaster here in Plymouth. Now that he had secured the services of Master George Renfield, he was on his way back and would guide the new teacher to Wethersfield.

The trader was a big, ruddy man with a swaggering manner and a friendly smile. A sword hung from the baldric that crossed the chest of his buff jacket. There was a brace of pistols thrust into his broad leather belt. His matchlock gun topped the load of the leading packhorse.

He doffed his hat to Goodwife Renfield across the fence and boomed a hearty good morning. Then his twinkling eyes lighted on Zeke's new gun. He nodded approvingly. "How did you come by a treasure like that, Son?" he asked.

"It's a present from my uncle." Zeke proudly offered the flintlock for inspection. "It's loaded," he cautioned as the trader looked it over.

"It's a marvelous weapon. The science of gun making is not likely to go far beyond a gun like this. I'll trade you five hundred beaver skins for it."

"No trade."

Master Elkins laughed. "I don't blame you, Son. Are you ready to start?" he added briskly.

"Quite ready," Zeke said.

His family clustered around him, everyone talking at once. His sister bussed him soundly; his brothers wrung his hand until it ached.

"Take good care of Uncle George," Roger grinned, as if Zeke were the oldster of the party.

Zeke's mother was looking from him to Judith, then Uncle George, as if she could not bear to see them go. From the anxious gleam in her eyes, Zeke knew that she was worrying about how they would make out in the wilderness, a boy, an absent-minded old gentleman, and a timid, city-bred little girl.

"I'll look out for them," he murmured.

She turned and hugged him tight in her arms. "I know you will. God bless you and keep you safe, my Zeke," she whispered.

He was afraid that he would disgrace himself by tears if he tried to say anything but "Goodbye, Mother."

His father came next with a hearty handshake, man to man.

"Go with God, my son."

Slow-footed Uncle George had already said his farewells and was trudging up the road bent beneath the weight of a sack containing more of his precious books.

Zeke charged about, driving Star and Marigold into the road. He slipped the armbands of his Indian pack basket over his shoulders, and then looked for Judith.

She was clinging to her aunt with one hand and to Tabby Paws with the other. Zeke gently drew her away from his mother. He took the kitten and handed it to Hope. "It's time to go, Judy," he said, pushing his dazed little cousin through the gate.

Hope ran after them, holding the kitten. "I'll bring Tabby Paws out to you next year, Judy!" she cried. "He'll be a fine big cat by then."

Judith couldn't answer for her tears. Zeke waved as cheerfully as he could. Then he and Judy were walking up the road. His musket lay on his arm; his other hand was leading Star. The horse was all but hidden beneath the pack. A peaked chicken coop topped the load, and every one of the six chickens inside was squawking its head off.

Up ahead, the bells on the pack train were dancing. Master Elkins was singing lustily as he tramped along.

Zeke turned once more to wave to his family, and then he faced staunchly ahead to where the forest began.

That morning they walked miles along a wooded road. Later they turned into a narrow trail that had been worn a foot deep by centuries of Indian travel to and from the coast.

"You must watch out for rattlesnakes, Mistress Judith," Master Elkins warned. "Do not step over a fallen tree without first scanning the ground on the other side. Serpents love to coil up on a bed of dry leaves against a log."

Judith looked frightened.

When shadows began to lengthen they made camp beside a clear little brook that threaded the vast forest of pines and hemlocks.

Judith plumped to the ground and pulled off her shoes to nurse her toes. Her father let down his sack of books with a sigh of relief. Zeke and Master Elkins removed the packs and tied the horses and cow in a grassy clearing along the brook.

While Master Elkins chopped wood for the fire, Zeke cut saplings and brush. The two of them made short work of building two brush shelters, a small one for Judith and a larger one for the rest of them. Inside there were springy beds of hemlock tips, piled up and interlaced until they formed a comfortable mattress.

Down by the brook, Marigold was lowing mournfully.

"It's milking time," Zeke hinted, pausing in his work to glance at Judith.

With a sigh she fetched a piggin and went timidly about the

business of milking. It was the first time she had attempted it without the supervision of Zeke's mother. Now nervousness made Judith so awkward that the irritated cow kicked over the piggin and wasted most of the milk. Shamefacedly Judith returned to the fire with the piggin less than half full.

"Never mind. You'll get the way of it soon," Zeke told her.

With a skill born of long familiarity with campfires, Master Elkins was stirring up a hasty pudding in an iron pot that stood among the coals on three squatty legs. From one of his packs he pulled two large wooden trenchers and four horn spoons. Into the trenchers he spooned liberal portions of pudding.

"That for you younkers," he said, handing one trencher to Zeke for him and Judith.

He placed the other on the ground between himself and Master Renfield.

Zeke fetched a box of maple sugar and poured milk from the piggin over the pudding. He thrust a spoon into Judith's hand.

Judith just sat there.

"Aren't you hungry?" he asked as he dug into their portion of pudding.

"Yes. But I want a plate to myself."

Master Elkins spoke up cheerfully from the other side of the fire. "It's nice to be elegant when there are enough dishes to go around."

Fingering her spoon, Judith sat by with up-tilted nose while Zeke enjoyed the pudding.

"Come on, Judy, this is good!" He added an extra sprinkling of maple sugar.

Judith licked her lips with the tip of her tongue. She dipped her spoon daintily into the trencher.

M-mm. The pudding was good, and she was very hungry after tramping all those miles.

She began to eat. "Zeke, stay on your own side of the dish!" she warned him, rapping his knuckles with her spoon when he pretended to steal some of her part of the pudding.

After supper Zeke and Master Elkins chopped enough wood to keep a blazing watch fire all night. Judith carried the dishes down to the brook to scour them with sand and rinse them with clear water.

Zeke heard a scream. Judith came scurrying back toward the fire.

He tore over to her. "What's wrong?"

"A rattle serpent!" she cried, clutching his arm. "Down there by the brook."

"Did it bite you?"

"I—I don't think so." She was shaking with fright.

Zeke blew out his breath in a gasp of relief.

"You'd know if it had. The pain is fearsome."

He picked up a stout stick and went cautiously down the bank.

"Over there," Judy directed, standing excitedly on tiptoe.

Zeke took one look at the little green snake and threw down his stick in disgust.

Bending down, he grasped the shimmering thing just behind its head. As he held it up, its slender length writhed and whipped around his wrist.

"Put it down before it bites you!" Judith begged.

"It's only a harmless little adder. Look, Judy!" He started toward her.

Judith backed away a few steps and then turned and ran.

Zeke raced after her, still holding the snake. "I tell you it won't hurt you!" he yelled. He grabbed her arm and pulled her around to face him. "You've got to learn to tell the harmless ones from the poisonous."

"No, no!" she jerked away and ran to her shelter.

Zeke tossed the snake into a bush and went back to the fire. "I guess I just don't understand girls," he said to Master Elkins.

He felt a pang of remorse as he pictured Judy crying in her shelter. Poor little girl, she was afraid of the woods to begin with; why had he tried to force her to look at the snake? Didn't Hope carry on in the same silly way if she saw him pick up a caterpillar? Yet it was important that Judith learn to live in the woods.

CHAPTER 3
Nemox

Next morning, before sunrise, Zeke awoke and sat for a while near the fire with his musket across his knees. At this eerie hour the camp seemed a lonesome place. Even the diamond bright stars looked more remote than those that had winked down from above the friendly roofs of Plymouth Town.

A resin-loaded log exploded in the fire and a cloud of sparks billowed skyward. Zeke looked around uneasily. It gave him a queer, lost feeling to think of what a tiny pin point of light this fire must make in all the leagues of a dark forest stretching on and on, until, perhaps, they reached the China Sea.

Something was making the horses restless. Zeke walked over to where the stock was tied to trees at the edge of the ring of firelight. He stroked Marigold's velvety muzzle and spoke to each of the horses soothingly. At the end of the line he walked a short way into the shadowy heart of the forest.

Beyond the fire glow, darkness flowed over him. For a moment he felt as though he were standing at the bottom of a deep, black pool. Then his eyes became accustomed to the gloom and he found that he could see quite well.

A light breeze stirred and whispered in the pines, bringing

with it the damp fresh breath of dawn. From the direction of camp came the merest ghost of a sound, but it was enough to alert Zeke to possible danger. He pressed close against a big tree, so that their shadows merged.

His eyes caught a swift movement and then made out an animal traveling through the woods with long, springy bounds. The creature's pointed nose was in the air, as if he were hot on the trail of some zestful scent that had come to him on the breeze.

Zeke could see him plainly now. He was dark furred and bush tailed, something like an enormous mink in build, yet larger and much more formidable than any mink. Every line of his long, muscular body and short, sturdy legs expressed speed and terrific fighting power.

Fisher-cat! Zeke eagerly followed every movement of the beautiful animal. He had heard many hunters' tales about the courage of the fisher-cat but this was the first time he had seen one alive.

The fisher-cat paused and glanced upward, still sniffing the air. Then he ran to a nearby pine and raced up the trunk with a light scratching of long claws on the bark.

A plump cock partridge was roosting behind a thin screen of needles on the lowest limb of this pine. Zeke saw the fisher-cat run out on the limb. The big, ruffed bird stirred in its sleep, but the fisher's long teeth closed on its neck and snuffed out its life before it came really awake.

The fisher-cat let the bird's heavy body tumble to the ground; then he streaked back along the limb and ran headfirst down the trunk of the pine. But before he could reach his kill, a lynx bounded out of a thicket and planted one bulky paw on the dead partridge.

Laying back his tasseled ears, the lynx let out a challenging screech full in the face of the oncoming fisher-cat.

The fisher-cat paused, but it was plain that he had no intention of allowing the lynx to steal his breakfast. He crouched low, his bushy tail swishing angrily. His lips drew back from gleaming teeth in a grin of fury. His eyes glowed red. With a thin, ravening snarl he rushed at the lynx.

Spitting and growling, the lynx, much larger than he, reared and slashed out like a boxer with a huge paw. The fisher-cat whisked aside so that the long claws merely raked his heavily muscled shoulder.

His teeth ripped across the face of the lynx, just missing an eye.

Yowling like a mad thing the lynx sprang at his enemy with claws spread wide. He was still in the air when the fisher-cat flashed in from below and clamped his incisors upon the lynx's throat. The fisher never let go that deepening throat hold throughout the rest of the fight.

Straining and rending the two rolled over and over in a flurry of slashing claws and tearing teeth.

Zeke was shaking with excitement and almost yelled out

as the lynx rolled on his back and strove to rip the belly of the fisher-cat with his terrible hind claws.

The lithe fisher eluded those raking claw strokes by throwing his body from side to side. Meanwhile the strength in his shoulders enabled him to bore in and pin the heavier lynx down with a throat hold—the merciless throat hold used by all the weasel kind.

The wheezing lynx was growing weaker, but he continued the struggle until the teeth of the fisher-cat finally met in his jugular vein. Then the long claws of the lynx spread and tightened in his furry pads. He lay still.

The fisher-cat stood over the dead foe for a moment. He himself was bleeding from a slash on his shoulder and from a deep wound where the lynx had clawed his flank.

"Whew!" Zeke passed the back of a shaky hand across his wet forehead.

At the sound of his voice the fisher whirled around and bared his teeth in a threatening snarl. As he met those blazing eyes, Zeke felt a rush of fear.

Hastily he aimed his musket at the crouching animal, but he lowered it again without firing.

The fisher-cat had fought the lynx in defense of what was his own. His courage in the face of great odds had earned him the right to live.

"Go in peace," Zeke told him softly.

He sighed with relief when the fisher-cat picked up the partridge in his jaws and backed slowly away.

"Thank you, Brother," said a voice close by.

Zeke spun around.

An Indian boy of about his own age was standing beside him.

"Koue," Zeke said. "Where did you come from?" He spoke in the Algonquin tongue, which he had learned from the many Indians who hunted and fished with the boys of Plymouth.

The strange boy did not answer until the fisher-cat had vanished among the trees, then he turned to Zeke.

"I followed Nemox here and watched him fight upweekis. It means good luck to me that Nemox won." The Indian stood straight and proud, holding a bow in one hand. "I am Nemox too. I took my name from him, Nemox, swiftest hunter in the woods."

Nemox. This was an Indian word that Zeke had not heard before. "Nemox in your language," he said. "Fisher-cat in mine. But I don't know why we call him fisher."

The Indian Nemox laughed. "He eats fish when he finds one. Fishing is too slow for Nemox. He fights. He hunts. On the ground and in the trees there is no hunter to match Nemox. And no warrior so brave." A smile lighted his copper-skinned face. "You aimed the fire stick at Nemox but you did not shoot."

"A warrior as brave as Nemox deserves to live," Zeke

explained.

Nemox lifted his arm in the Indian gesture of friendship.

There was a warm feeling around Zeke's heart as he in turn lifted his arm.

"Brother," Nemox asked, "how are you named in your own tongue?"

"Zeke Renfield."

"You do not shoot Nemox," Nemox said gravely, "and for that we are friends."

Zeke now noticed the design on the boy's deerskin shirt. It was the head of a wolf, or as the Indian would say, Mohegan!

"I must follow Nemox," Nemox said. "Hijah, Zeke Renfield." He turned and was off in long, soft strides.

"Hijah, Nemox," Zeke called after him.

Zeke watched him disappear. He wished that he had thought to invite the Mohegan boy to breakfast. And he wished also he could see Roger and Alan. Wouldn't their eyes open, though, when he'd tell them about this next year!

CHAPTER 4
Fair Trade

Judith took the piggin and went gingerly about milking Marigold. But she managed better this morning. When she returned to the fire she filled a noggin with milk for Zeke.

"Thank you, Judy!" he said, accepting it with glad surprise. Maybe she had the makings of a pioneer after all, and he told her so.

She looked up at Zeke and Master Elkins, her eyes filled with wonderment at the idea. "But can a person who's afraid," she asked, "become a pioneer?"

"Surely!" Master Elkins laughed with a roar. "I'm afraid sometimes. But on I must go."

"Well, I had a little scare this morning," Zeke said, and he told of his encounter with the two Nemoxes.

When Zeke had finished, the trader said, "Lad, your friend Nemox is the nephew of a great chief, the Sachem of the Mohegans. When they fight they are the fiercest of the tribes. It is well to have them for friends."

"It is well to have all men for friends," Master Renfield put in, looking up from a book.

"Aye, that is true, sir," Master Elkins replied, "and that is just what the Sachem Uncas believes. He is a shrewd man. I've traded with him, and I know. He tries to keep peace with the other Indians, and at the same time is doing all he can to stay on good terms with the Owanux—which they call us English. But if he ever turns against us, we had better all go back to England, if we can get away alive."

"Will his nephew become Sachem some day?" Zeke wondered.

"That, or a Sagamore," the trader answered. "You did a fine morning's work, Zeke. Nemox is probably on an errand for his uncle right now, to Plymouth, to learn more about the Owanux ways. And you're one Owanux he's learned something from already."

"What could that be, Master Elkins?"

"That some of us Owanuxes are not afraid to play fair, as you did with the fisher-cat."

Judith looked at her cousin very earnestly. "Zeke," she said, "please, will you find me another little snake? Maybe if I make myself hold it I won't be afraid of it anymore."

"That I will," Zeke said, chuckling, "but the main thing is, Judy, to learn the difference between the good snakes and the poisonous ones."

One morning many days later, a gaunt Indian appeared abruptly from the trees ahead.

Master Elkins snatched his matchlock off the packhorse and blew on the smoldering end of the fuse. Zeke quickly bunched the stock and motioned to his uncle and cousin to get behind trees.

A dumpy little squaw stepped into the trail beside her man. On seeing her, the Owanuxes relaxed, except Judith, who crowded close to her father.

Master Elkins lifted his arm in friendly greeting, and Zeke did likewise. "Koue!" they called ahead.

"Koue," the brave replied in a quiet tone. He carried a bow and a flint-headed fish spear. His wife held a bulky deerskin sack in one hand and a bundle of fur in the other.

Evidently they had been out on a long trip of hunting and trapping, or were moving from winter to summer quarters. Zeke noticed that they had stepped out of a narrow, scarcely distinct cross-trail that continued somewhat in the same westerly direction as the one his own party was on, except that it cut a little more southward.

"Are you alone with your wife and child?" the trader asked in Algonquin.

"Yes, Friend," the brave replied in the same tongue.

On the little squaw's back rode a plump papoose in a birchbark cradle.

Judith now was at ease and came forward for a closer look at the beady-eyed baby Indian.

The squaw carried also a bulky deerskin sack and a large bundle of fur.

Master Elkins pointed to the fur and said in English, "You trade?"

"I trade."

The brave told his squaw to open the bundle. Wordlessly she spread out the skins of beaver and otter and richly-furred fisher-cat.

The trader picked up another skin. He stroked the soft fur, blew on it.

"Good fur," the Indian said. "What you give?"

Master Elkins opened one of his packs. He held up a small sack of bright beads, then a brass kettle.

"Wah," the brave said, unimpressed. No, he did not want these. "Gun? Rum?"

"No gun and no rum," Master Elkins answered.

Then out of the back he pulled an azure coat.

"Gun," the brave insisted.

"Wah," the trader countered.

Judith went closer to the fat, happy papoose. "Koue," she said.

Zeke noticed this and was pleased. It was the first Indian word she had uttered in her life.

"Good, Judy!" he whispered, and then nodded to the squaw, who was hardly taller than she. "My cousin admires your beautiful baby," he said in Algonquin.

The little squaw returned the admiration by staring round-eyed at the pink plumes on Judith's hat.

Judith's eyes went down to the squaw's comfortable looking moccasins. Her own shoes were worn through. All their fancy appearance was gone.

So, while Zeke was busy with stock, Judith tried to deal with the squaw. She pointed down to her worn shoes and made a face of agony. Then she pointed to the moccasins and smiled, thumping herself on the chest to show how proud she would be to have them. "Ugh?"

The little woman looked surprised and obligingly repeated "Ugh, ugh."

But she did not understand until after Judith had gone through several more attempts at sign language.

Finally, the woman's face lighted up and she nodded. She dove into her deerskin sack and brought out a new pair of moccasins. They had flaps at the ankle and were embroidered with green and yellow porcupine quills. Beaming, she waved them before the little Owanux girl. Then she jabbed a stubby finger at the plumed hat and made as if she were placing a hat on her own head.

A few minutes later when the conference broke up and the Indian couple plodded off down the cross-trail, Zeke chanced to gaze back at them. "Hi Judy," he exclaimed. "That squaw's walking off with your hat!"

"And I'm walking off with her shoes," Judith answered, striding lightly ahead.

"Now, that is excellent," Master Elkins said. "For those two with whom we've now dealt are Wongunks, your future neighbors. They live downriver from Wethersfield."

"Then we must be not distant from it, ourselves," Master Renfield observed.

Thus far on the trip he had plodded ahead of Zeke, uncomplaining, silent, deep in his own thoughts, confidently letting the trader lead the march while his nephew brought up the rear. Now he looked about him at the new country.

The long journey came to an end on the bank of a broad river, as blue as the sky above it.

"Wethersfield!" Pride rang in Bejoyful Elkins' voice. He pointed across the water, and started the horses down the slope of the river.

The others stood still a moment, staring across at their new home. Over the sun-spangled water they could see green meadows that stretched back to rolling hills, where the forest began again. There were dark patches of plowed fields with people at work in them. Cattle grazed in the riverside meadows. Log cabins were clustered near a log fort.

The Renfields now hurried after their guide, who explained:

"My friend, John Oldham, and I discovered yon stretch of natural meadowland while we were hunting and exploring in the valley. The Wongunk tribe used to have their ceremonial dances there. They called it 'Pyquog,' which means 'level ground good for a dancing place.'"

He then stepped into a thicket and pulled out a canoe which the settlers kept hidden on that side of the river for the use of travelers. "You stay and watch the cattle, Zeke. I'll set Master Renfield and Judith across the river and come back with a raft."

CHAPTER 5

The Renfield Pocconock

No more work was done that day in Wethersfield. It was months since the people there had seen anyone from the outside world. And Bejoyful Elkins with his jovial manner was a favorite with them. Everybody, child or adult, called him by his first name, "Bejoyful! Bejoyful!"

They crowded into his cabin to welcome the new schoolmaster. Those who could not wedge their way inside flocked around the doors and windows, craning their necks to see and hear what was going on.

After Bejoyful finished answering their many questions about the latest doings back in Plymouth, their new schoolmaster amazed them with news that was only a little more than three months old from far-off England, about King Charles' activities.

The women and the girls made much over Judith's dress. It was torn by brambles, scorched by cooking fires, spotted with mud and grease. To them, though, it was still a London gown, made in the latest style and of finest cloth. The homespun womenfolk stroked it with their work-roughened hands and wistfully fingered what was left of the silk galloon trimming.

After a few days of rest from the journey, Master Renfield and his nephew were ready to look around for a suitable home site. Although the Colony was only two years old, they would have to go some distance from the settlement to find a piece of land with plenty of room, the kind of soil that John Renfield had told his son to look for if he could find it, and plenty of wood nearby.

"We shall have to purchase it from the Wongunks," Bejoyful said. "And I am the man to help with that, for I was with the party that purchased Pyquog from their Chief, old Sequin."

On the way down to the Wongunk village, he explained to Master Renfield and Zeke that at one time all the land thereabout had belonged to the Wongunks.

"But there's a warlike tribe that call themselves Pequots, which I'm told means 'fox-like destroyers.' If so, the rascals are well-named. Well, these fox-like Pequots have annoyed and bullied the mild and amiable Wongunks so much that these folk are glad to have us English colonists around to protect them."

"Little though we can, Master Elkins?" Zeke's uncle asked.

"Well, sir, we have firearms, and you have already had occasion to observe how much the Indian respects and covets them."

The trail they were following dropped down off the wooded highlands and angled across rich alluvial meadows to the river. Indian women were working garden patches with clamshell hoes and rakes made of moose antlers. One woman was wearing a pink plumed hat tilted saucily on her braided hair. Zeke smiled to her and waved his hand. He got a friendly flourish of her hoe in reply.

In one garden, set apart from the others, only men were working.

"That's the tobacco patch," Bejoyful explained. "Tobacco is the only crop a warrior will tend."

A group of dignified older men were seated on the margin of the tobacco field smoking their clay pipes while they watched the young warriors at work.

Bejoyful walked up to a thick-set Indian whose tawny-red face was covered with a network of wrinkles.

"Greetings, Sequin." Bejoyful said in Algonquin, and made the peace sign.

"Brother, I greet you," the Wongunk Sachem said.

Over their pipes the other Indians watched the visitors with alert dark eyes.

Bejoyful waved his hand toward Master Renfield. "My brothers would trade for Wongunk land."

Sequin stared gravely at the Renfields. "Sit!" he said at last.

All three seated themselves cross-legged on the ground in front of him.

Sequin puffed solemnly, and then handed the pipe to Bejoyful. The trader took a long, slow pull and handed it back.

Sequin smoked again. It was Master Renfield's turn next. He accepted the pipe in his dignified manner and placed the clay stem in his mouth.

Zeke squirmed uneasily. He would be next! What if it made him sick and he disgraced himself before all these Indians? He wondered desperately how his uncle managed to look as though he enjoyed smoking a pipe that the old Chief had just removed from his mouth.

Master Renfield finished his smoke and returned the pipe to Sequin.

Once more the Sachem smoked while Zeke watched nervously. Gravely Sequin offered the pipe to him.

Zeke noted that the bowl of clay was molded in the form of a grotesque bear's head. He put the stem between his teeth and drew a long breath upon it. Smoke filled his lungs and the sweetly acrid taste of tobacco bit his tongue.

"Well done," Bejoyful murmured into his ear.

Having performed the rite of hospitality, Sequin laid his pipe aside.

There followed a silence that Zeke thought would last forever.

Finally the Sachem spoke.

"Where land?"

Bejoyful took a pointed stick and drew a map upon the

ground. Here Wethersfield, there the Wongunk camp. He placed an X between them. "Here. Enough for two homesteads."

Sequin conferred seriously with the other Indians.

"What pay?" he asked, turning back to Bejoyful.

Zeke opened the pack they had brought with them. He laid out a brass kettle, some hand mirrors, bags of beads and cheap jewelry, an ax, some small knives, and two bolts of cloth, one scarlet, one emerald green.

The Wongunks were delighted. Sequin expressed himself as being well pleased with this payment for the large tract of land.

Zeke's first task was to build two brush shelters. He also made a stone fireplace, with a lugpole of green wood for Judith to latch the pothooks to.

The shelters stood near a spring on a grassy open terrace, shaded by lofty elm trees. So the forest pressed close. In front, though, a sweet-scented meadow stretched down to the river. Here the Wongunks had once planted corn. Zeke hitched Star to the plow and broke up part of the old field for his own crop.

Next day Bejoyful drove a yoke of oxen over from the village to help with the plowing. And at noon Judith brought out a basket of food to make a picnic under the elm.

Zeke stooped down and picked up a fistful of dark earth. The smell of it was damp and cool, and yet it held the sun's warmth too.

"Noble stuff, lad," Bejoyful reflected, "and the maize you'll get from it will be sweet."

"This is as fair a meadow as ever I saw in the Old Country," Uncle George said.

"I like it better, Father," Judy said. "Never have I seen a place as pretty as this."

"It is a pretty pocconock," Bejoyful agreed.

"Pocconock, pocconock." Judith enjoyed the Algonquin word as much as the food they were eating.

"Aye, Judy," Zeke said, "to think the Renfield's now own a pocconock, a pretty pocconock, on the Connecticut River!"

Zeke grew gaunt and hard as he toiled from sunup till dusk through the long days of spring and summer. At first his uncle made a few efforts to help, but after he almost cut off his toe while splitting kindling, he returned to his books.

Zeke carried the full, heavy load of responsibility, but felt freer and happier than he had ever been in his life.

One day a group of neighbors came over from the village to help the Renfields raise their cabin. The ring of many axes sounded in the woods, and tall trees came crashing down. With so many hands to help, the framework of the cabin was soon up and the walls began to rise, log on log. Zeke notched logs, a task at which he was quick and skillful. Judith helped to chink the spaces between the logs with moss and clay.

After their friends had gone away, the three Renfields went into the empty cabin, where the clean, piney smell of fresh-cut logs hung pleasantly on the air.

Zeke fetched wood and made the first fire in the huge fireplace. "It draws well," he said happily as the flames leaped up.

He looked around the one large room and thought of all the things still to be done. He must make a bed in the loft for Judith, bunks downstairs for himself and Uncle George, shelves, wooden shutters for the windows, stools, a table… It was a good thing that he had learned to handle tools well in his father's woodworking shop.

Fortunately, he had helpful neighbors. Gid Ash, a boy of his own age, lived nearest. He and Gid were back and forth between the Renfield and the Ash pocconocks, and so he didn't look forward with dread to cutting the hay in the wild meadows while good weather held. Judy would lend a hand to the corn harvesting. She still burned food and her cooking was sometimes not easy to eat. But it was improving, thanks also to neighbors, Goodwife Ash and Goodwife Barns.

One night Bejoyful and Zeke stood talking outside the cabin.

"Hear that?" Bejoyful cocked his head toward the October moon.

"Honk Honka Honk Honka Honk"

Zeke nodded. For days he had been hearing that sky music of wild geese winging their way south.

Bejoyful folded his arms and winked. "Will Muzzy and

Holdfast Barns are going with me on a hunting trip in a cove a long way downriver where wild rice grows. Could you spare the time to join us, Zeke?"

"There's much to do…" Zeke answered, struggling between his urgent autumn work and this challenging call that came out of the high sky.

Uncle George stepped through the doorway. "Ezekiel," he said quietly, "game fowl is food too. And even though it were only for the sport of it, I wish you would go with Master Elkins on this hunt."

"Good counsel, sir," Bejoyful said stoutly. He patted Zeke on both arms. "And now, my lad, get yourself to bed and be up to meet us at the village wharf in two turns of the hourglass."

CHAPTER 6
Trout for Breakfast

The moon was hanging low above the western hills when the shallop dropped anchor off a densely wooded point of land that jutted out into the water on the east bank of the river. Inside the point Zeke could see the moon-washed waters of the deep cove. He and the others got into a smaller boat and rowed ashore.

Bejoyful, Holdfast Barns, and Will Muzzy were armed with matchlock guns. Besides a rest on which to prop the gun for firing, each carried a length of slow-burning match, or rope, with which to touch the blunderbuss off. Their ammunition hung in little metal cylinders from the bandoliers that crossed their chests. Every time they moved, the cylinders would jingle and tinkle until Zeke wondered why every wild goose south of Wethersfield had not long since taken flight.

Bejoyful told his companions to find hiding places in the reeds at some distance apart from one another. Zeke went first, making his way along the marshy shoreline of the cove by jumping from one hummock to another. He landed on a grassy mound that was larger and firmer than most, then realized he had stumbled upon an abandoned muskrat lodge hidden in the reeds. From its top he had a good view of the open waters of the cove. It was an ideal place from which to shoot geese.

A chilly mist rose from the water. Zeke now crouched down in the long grass on top of the muskrat lodge and pulled a corner of his jacket over the lock on his musket to keep it dry. The ghostly silence made him feel as though he were alone in the gray, dripping world.

The first pale light of dawn glimmered in the east. Small stirrings and splashings began to come from different parts of the cove. Out from shore a gander raised his head and greeted the day with a sonorous honking.

Rent by the warmth of the rising sun, the mist floated away in ragged streamers. Zeke could see the geese now, so many of them that it was scarcely necessary to take aim. He brought up his gun and fired. At the same instant there were three more explosions of smoke and flame to his left.

Those old hand-cannons, Zeke thought as he reloaded his gun. He poured in powder, thumped the butt on the ground; he dropped in the shot, wadded it down, snapped the lock to prime it, and was the first to fire a second shot. The clumsy matchlocks took much longer to load.

The first fusillade had spread panic among the geese and sent them flapping into the air. Their harsh, terrified honking echoed over the cove.

Bang! Bang! Bang!

Heavy black and gray birds fell with a splash into the water. All the rest of the flock was in the air now, some circling the cove, others winging skyward in the wake of the leader. Swiftly they were beyond musket range.

Zeke couldn't see Bejoyful but he heard his hearty voice behind the wall of reeds.

"Keep your places, boys. I'll row around in the boat and collect the birds. Then we'll fix a decoy and wait for another flock to come over."

"Wait for us!" shouted Will Muzzy. "We left our lunch in the boat."

Zeke heard the three of them calling to each other as they picked their way to the point of land where they had left the rowboat.

Judith had given him a large square of cornbread spread with butter and blackberry preserve. The bread was soggy but Zeke ate it hungrily.

Then as he turned to lie back in comfort his elbow struck the flintlock and sent it sliding down the side of the lodge. He grabbed it as it struck the water but not quickly enough to prevent it from getting wet. Muttering at his own carelessness, he started to open the lock, but heard people yelling. It seemed to be over at the point. Forgetting the wet gun in his hand he sat a moment listening.

Somebody's matchlock thundered, and frenzied screeches followed. He felt a stab of fright.

Indian war whoops?

He threw himself flat in the grass with his useless gun

clutched in one hand.

There was more firing at the point, more shouting. A breeze rustled the reeds, parting them gently, so he could see across the waters of the cove to where the wooded point thrust its rocky tip out into the river. Will and Holdfast were clambering into the boat. Bejoyful was behind a tree, firing at something hidden on the land side of the point.

Zeke's scalp prickled. Hostile Indians in the woods could easily shoot him full of arrows if he made a dash to join his friends.

They were probably in worse danger than he. And here he was, with the best gun of the lot, unable to fire a shot to aid them. All because of his own carelessness!

The reeds bent again. He saw the boat in the water with Holdfast dragging Will over the side. There was an arrow sticking in Will's shoulder.

Bejoyful plunged heavily down the bank and splashed to the boat. A tomahawk whizzed past his head. Then half a dozen Indians burst out of the trees. Just as the reeds swayed together Zeke heard a single shot. He guessed that Holdfast had fired at the Indians while Bejoyful climbed into the boat.

He had a better view of the boat when it pulled into deep water and headed into the cove. A flight of arrows sped after it but did no harm. Then the boat was beyond bowshot.

"Zeke!" shouted Bejoyful.

He was answered by a chorus of yells from the Indians as they raced around to that side of the point.

"Where are you, Zeke?" Bejoyful bawled. "Swim for it. We'll come in for you."

But Zeke dared not betray his whereabouts to the Indians. He slid into the water and cowered there in the shelter of the tall reeds.

Bejoyful repeated his summons.

The Indians evidently thought that the big Englishman was yelling insults at them. They jumped up and down in rage. "English are afraid to fight!" they howled in Algonquin. "English warriors run away like women!"

Again they filled the air with arrows; some of these went uncomfortably close to the boat, which slowly pulled out of the cove and headed for the shallop.

With a heavy heart Zeke watched his friends board the shallop. It was all he could do to stifle a yell as Holdfast hoisted the anchor.

They were going away! They were leaving him with the Indians!

As the sail filled and the boat disappeared around a bend in the river, Zeke felt as if he would whimper like a sick, deserted puppy. Instead, he pressed his tense body deeper into the water and the mud.

He could hear the Indians diving into the water when they

went to swim out and gather in the geese. Afterward, puffs of smoke came across the cove from a fire. He could smell roasting geese and broiling venison. Evidently these Indians were a hunting party and had already got a deer.

His body was one chilly ache. He wondered miserably how much longer he could hold out.

After a few moments of strained watching, he struggled out of his muddy bed and crawled up the sloping side of the mound where the muskrat lodge was. He lay face down in the long grass.

Hours seemed to pass. He was so hungry he could have devoured a mud turtle raw.

He realized there had not been a noise from the point across the cove for a long time. Except for the whisper of the reeds down near the water, not a sound broke the stillness. He rose stiffly on his cramped legs. His feet in the slimy wet moccasins felt like cakes of ice. He stamped them, flapped his arms, rubbed his hands together.

As soon as he could use his fingers he eagerly examined his gun. It was hopelessly wet.

He drew the useless charge and tried to dry the lock with his woolen cap. Fortunately, he had left the powder horn and cartridge box lying here on top of the muskrat mound, and they were dry. He took a small square of linen he kept in the box and used it with the ramrod to swab out the damp barrel. If only he dared make a fire to dry it!

It was twilight now. Venturing out of his hiding place, he made his way cautiously around the marshy shore of the cove to the higher ground at the point.

The swift patter of feet and a whiff of musky scent told him that a fox had been there before him, prowling around the remains of the Indians' banquet. The fox probably wouldn't have come here if there were still any of the men about.

He found that the heap of ashes in the big fireplace was still warm. After the long hours in the water the feel of warm, soft wood ashes between his fingers was irresistible. He could not tear himself from this source of heat, even though he feared he should be getting away from here.

He hung his powder horn and cartridge box upon one of the pines that ringed the fireplace. The gun he laid carefully across two stones where it would benefit from the heat of the ashes. He took off his moccasins and stockings and spread them on stones to dry. Finally he plunged his feet into the ashes, which reached above his ankles.

"Ahh!" he breathed, squatting down to get every bit of the delicious warmth.

He ran his fingers through the heap of bones that were scattered around the fireplace and came upon a rib bone with a little meat and fat still sticking to it. As he brought it to his mouth he remembered the foraging fox. He wiped the bone on the sleeve of his jacket. Too hungry to be finicky, he soon was gnawing away.

If Judith with her dainty table manners could only see him now, wallowing in these ashes and gnawing a bone that was the leavings of some oily savage, and that had probably been mouthed by a fox as well!

The ashes were growing cold. As the lopsided autumn moon began to climb above the trees Zeke decided that he must be on his way.

He pulled on his partly dried hose and his moccasins. The heat had dried the lock and barrel of his gun. He wiped it and greased it carefully. Finally he loaded it.

Following the river north would be the simplest way of getting home, but he figured that there was a greater risk of meeting Indians near the river. He decided to strike inland before he turned north.

Several hours later he found himself following up a brook that led him into a narrow valley between two low ridges. Huge boulders were heaped up and tumbled together here in vast confusion.

The moon was clouded. Soon its light would be gone, and travel through this rough country would be almost impossible.

There were many dark openings of caves in the rocks. Zeke chose a shallow one behind a screen of bushy hemlocks. Here, with his back to the rocks, he might rest fairly secure until morning.

The sun was above the treetops now. The brook glinted golden brown under the hemlock. Zeke sprawled on a flat rock and peered into the deep water of a big pool. A school of small fish, darting past like shadows, scattered in frantic haste as a big brook trout shot out from beneath the rock. Zeke sucked in his breath. Here was his breakfast—if he could catch it!

He dug in his breeches pocket for the homespun fish line he always carried wrapped around a large hook. With his sheath knife he dug for worms beneath a rotting log. There were more than enough.

He crept back to the rock and tossed the baited hook into the pool. Almost instantly he felt a violent tug. He set the hook sharply. The surface of the pool was shattered into crystal splinters as the huge trout curved upward in a glistening leap, then struck the water with a resounding slap of its square tail and dived deep into the pool. Zeke hauled in line as fast as he could. The fish broke water again, leaping and threshing.

"Hold, line! Hold!" he pleaded.

Hand over hand he dragged the fish out of the boiling water and up the face of the rock. He dropped it in a bed of ferns and killed it with a quick blow. Its colors had not yet faded. Even in his hunger Zeke had to admire the vivid spots of gold and violet and vermilion that glowed on its silken olive-green sides.

Beneath a tangle of grapevines he kindled a tiny, smokeless fire, lighting it with a spark from the flint on his musket. He spitted the trout on a green stick and laid it across two forked sticks set upright above the coals. While it was broiling he ate some grapes. When the trout was ready, he ate every bit of the firm, pink flesh and picked the bones. Finally he put out the fire beneath a smother of moss and went on his way along the brook.

CHAPTER 7
Pet Panther

Zeke climbed out of the valley, up the rocky flank of a roaring cataract of white water. Above it stretched a large beaver meadow. Setting his course by the sun, he started north through the hardwood forest that fringed the beaver pond.

Presently he had an uneasy feeling of being followed. He slipped behind a tree and stared back along his trail. Except for falling leaves nothing moved in the painted forest. He went on, still nagged by that spied-on feeling.

Soon he heard the calling of wild turkeys up ahead. He crept toward the glade where a flock of them were feeding on beech mast. Inching behind a screen of laurel, he bellied down, scarcely daring to breathe lest he alarm the weary, keen-eyed birds.

They "put-putted," scratched, and gobbled as they fed closer and closer to where Zeke was hiding.

He picked a royal looking gobbler and took aim. Before he could squeeze the trigger a big panther flashed across his vision and struck down that very bird. The rest of the flock scurried off, squawking with fright.

With the turkey in his mouth the panther turned blazing yellow eyes upon Zeke, as if defying him to do anything about it. Almost choking with disappointment and rage, Zeke trained the sight of his musket on the beast's broad nose.

Someone knocked the musket away so that it exploded harmlessly skyward. Then strong arms gripped Zeke.

A tawny-red face with glittery black eyes came around. It looked vaguely familiar. It was the Mohegan boy!

"Well for you, well for all the English that you did not slay the panther of Matchit-Moodus," he said severely in Algonquin.

Zeke gave Nemox an angry, puzzled look.

"Brother, in friendship I spoiled your shot," Nemox continued. "Had you killed him, Ninigret would have roused every tribe in valley to war against the English."

"Who is Ninigret?"

"She is the Wise Woman. My great-grandmother. She belongs to us, the Wolf People. But the Fox people and all the other tribes heed her. For she is the only person that Hobomoko will speak to. He is terrible. He is the god of thunder. He is very terrible, sometimes evil," Nemox shuddered.

"Then why do good Indian people wish to hearken to him?" Zeke asked in Algonquin so broken that Nemox winced and smiled.

"This why, Zeke Renfield," he replied in equally broken English. "Hobomoko very strong. He make big thunder noise from high sky. He make thunder noise from deep inside ground. Rr-rr-rr-rr-agh!" Nemox pointed downward. "He make evil noise, in cave where live Ninigret. We say it, 'Matchit-Moodus.' He speak to Ninigret."

"But if it is evil, why do you heed him?"

"We heed Ninigret. She the Wise Woman. She hear evil from Hobomoko and tell what will be good. We do like she say, is wise. Is good medicine-luck. We do not, is bad medicine."

Nemox turned to look at the panther that had already finished his meal and was washing his face like a big housecat.

My turkey! Zeke thought resentfully as he saw the blowing feathers. He was hungry.

The young panther licked his furry sides with a lazy pink tongue while Nemox told him gravely to return at once to Matchit-Moodus. His golden eyes glinted from one human to the other. He stood up. As he yawned and stretched, muscles rippled like music beneath his sleek coat. Then he padded off into the thicket.

Nemox was obviously relieved. "Loks will sleep now. Then he will return to Moodus. Ninigret raised him from a kitten. There are not guns or copper kettles enough in all the English towns to trade for him."

Zeke thought that no one would be likely to trade for Loks unless it was to make a rug of him.

"How does he come to be so far from home, Nemox?"

"I am on an errand northward for Ninigret and I have let him follow part way. But what are you doing in these parts, Zeke Renfield?"

In a few words Zeke told him of the Indian attack. He could see that Nemox was not surprised.

"They were Pequots," Nemox said, picking up his bow of sassafras wood.

"But why would they attack us? We were not on their land." Zeke was too excited to speak Algonquin.

"Pequots hate all Owanux," Nemox replied calmly in English as he slung over his shoulder a quiver of arrows tufted with blue jay feathers. "Come, Brother. I guide you back to Pyquog."

Without another word or glance he started off through the forest. Zeke looked after him a moment and followed.

After they had gone several miles Nemox paused and dropped down behind a log. Zeke immediately flattened out beside him.

Nemox touched Zeke's musket. "Be ready."

From a pouch at his belt Nemox took the wing bone of a turkey. Putting it to his mouth he made a sound like a turkey's gobble. For a moment they lay in tense stillness. Then Nemox called again. He kept this up until they heard an answering "put-put" far off in the woods.

Once more Nemox called. The turkey answered—and more than one. This time the birds were closer, but their colors blended so perfectly with the autumn woods that only the occasional flutter of a wing enabled Zeke to keep track of them. Some of the flock drifted slowly along the ground, some flew from limb to limb in the wide-spreading oaks. All kept stretching out their necks as they peered ahead in an effort to sight the strange "bird" that had called them up.

When the turkeys were close enough for a shot, Nemox nudged Zeke who rose swiftly to one knee and aimed at a plump hen. The musket spat smoke and lead. The flock scattered in squawking confusion, all but the hen Zeke had shot through the head.

Nemox gave Zeke an approving glance.

Zeke gathered dry wood and made a fire. Nemox used his flint tomahawk to cut off the head and wings of the turkey and prepare it for roasting. From a nearby brook he fetched clay which he smeared in a thick coat over the unplucked bird. Placing the bulky clay bundle among the glowing coals, he built the fire up over it.

While their dinner was cooking, Nemox took from the deerskin pouch at his belt a cake of cornmeal and ground roasted chestnuts. He offered this to Zeke and brought out another for himself.

Zeke sampled the cake dubiously. But it was delicious. "Good!" he exclaimed.

Nemox's strong teeth flashed in a pleased smile. "White men's bread is good too," he said.

"You ate English bread at Plymouth," Zeke guessed. "I wish you could give me word of my folks."

"I did not stay long in English town," Nemox told him. "Uncas sent a runner for me in the Moon of Berries. Uncas thought there would soon be trouble between the English and Indians."

"We English hope not," Zeke said in his friend's language. "Why do the Pequots hate us? We've done them no harm."

"They think you have," Nemox said, his face becoming a smooth mask of copper. "Somebody at an upriver trading post killed their Sachem."

With a pang of dread, Zeke thought of Judy and Uncle George alone and probably helpless on the isolated farm. He pictured a black heap of ashes where the cabin had been, his folks killed or taken prisoner. Why, oh why had he gone hunting and left them? Yet he was unwilling to betray his fear to Nemox, who now rose to his feet and stood facing him across the fire.

Although Nemox was not yet old enough for a warrior's plume, he very proudly wore the iridescent turkey feather of a hunter in his hair. The Wolf Head of the Royal Clan glittered in purple wampum upon the front of his fringed tunic. Upon his deerskin pouch the likeness of a fisher-cat was embroidered in rare black shells.

As if reading his thoughts, Nemox said, "There is yet peace between our people."

"And between you and me," Zeke said, holding out his hand impulsively.

"Peace between you and me, Brother."

They shook hands solemnly.

Nemox turned away then and found a stick with which to poke the bundle of clay out of the fire. When he broke away the clay, feathers and skin came with it, leaving the well-cooked turkey meat.

Toward sunset they climbed a ridge and saw the Connecticut River gleaming between the wooded hills to westward.

Nemox stopped beneath a wind-twisted cedar, where a faint trail crossed the ridge from east to west. "Go toward the setting sun, Brother. Moonrise will find you close to Pyquog."

From his belt Nemox took the deerskin pouch and held it out to Zeke. One dark finger tapped the fisher-cat made of shell. "For you," he said in English. "You aim fire stick but you not shoot Nemox. I not forget."

Zeke spoke his thanks. Then he unbuckled his own belt and slipped off his sheath knife. Long and keen bladed, it would be a priceless possession to an Indian who had never owned anything but flint weapons and tools.

"Brother, wear this for me."

The black eyes glittered. "I thank you," he said proudly as befitted a future Sagamore of the Mohegans. Probably not even Uncas, their Sachem, owned such a knife as this.

Nemox attached the sheath to his own belt, and then lifted his arm in a gesture of farewell. "Netops, Zeke Renfield!"

"Hijah, Nemox!"

CHAPTER 8

Move Away!

The cabin was dark. Zeke hammered on the door. "Judy! Open up. It's Zeke!"

Inside there was a cry followed by a sound as if Judith had fallen over a stool. She clawed wildly at the bar, the door flew open, and she threw herself on him, almost knocking him breathless. "Zeke—Zeke! It's really you!"

"It surely is, Judy." His laugh was a little choked. "Aren't you going to let me in?"

She took his hand and dragged him inside.

He saw that she was crying. "Hi! Are you sorry to see me?"

Uncle George seized Zeke's hand and pumped it up and down. "Ezekiel, my dear boy! God be thanked!"

The lump in Zeke's throat made it difficult for him to reply. "It—it's good to be back, Uncle George."

He turned away abruptly and went to stand his gun in the corner.

"Oh, Zeke," Judith sobbed, "we-we, everybody, thought the Indians had—"

"And I thought they'd killed Bill Muzzy," Zeke replied. For it was only when he'd arrived at the Wethersfield landing that he heard of Will's arrow wound not being very bad. "Well, Will's mending," he said, picking up his cousin's hand and patting it, "and I-I'm fair starving."

The small hand was no longer the soft white one that had left Plymouth last spring, but tan and rough and scarred.

In her hurry to get him some supper, Judith stumbled over the stool again. She latched a kettle of cold bean porridge to the lug pole.

Zeke took off his jacket and scrubbed his face and hands at the wash bench by the door, all the while giving her and his uncle the main facts of his escape and return. "But everything I went through was worth it," he said, bringing the gift pouch over to his uncle. "I met my Mohegan friend again, the Fisher-Cat."

As he told this part of the story, Judith's fingers went over the black-shell embroidery of the fisher's head. She sighed over its beauty.

"It is indeed a symbol of friendship," Master Renfield said, "this pouch with his own totem on it. And Ezekiel, you say that he gave this gift first—simply gave it?"

"That was the way of it, sir," Zeke nodded. "It wasn't a trade between us. And when I gave him my knife, it was because I wanted him to have it from me."

As Judith bustled past Zeke he snitched a piece of cake from one of the platters she was carrying. "Zooks," he said chewing his first bite of it, "this is good cake, Judy!"

She beamed. "I gathered the nuts at the edge of our wood, and Gid brought us the wild honey I sweetened it with."

After his supper, Zeke learned why his uncle was so impressed with the friendship gift from an Indian.

"Master Elkins was here this afternoon with bad news. A sloop came up from Saybrook bringing word that the Pequots have killed his friend John Oldham."

Zeke was shocked out of his drowsiness. "How? Where?"

"Master Oldham set out in his sailboat to trade with the Indians on Block Island. The Indians pursued him in their canoes and murdered him."

"It's unfair!" Zeke was angry. He remembered what Nemox had told him: that the Pequots now hated all white folk because upriver somebody had killed their Sachem. "Master Oldham was probably nowhere around at the time their Sachem was killed."

"No. He was killed in a brawl at a Dutch trading post," Master Renfield said, "and John Oldham was as guiltless of it as any of us sitting here."

Weary as Zeke was, he did not rest easily that night.

The next day a town meeting was called. The people of Wethersfield were deeply incensed over the murder of the man who had founded their town. This and the attack on the hunting party at Wild Goose Cove was probably but the first of the outrages they had to fear from the new Pequot Sachem, Sassacus.

Bejoyful Elkins offered a motion that armed guards be posted on every trail leading to Wethersfield and that the friendly Wongunks be stationed on the ridges, from where they could use smoke to signal the settlement at the first sign of hostile Indians.

This motion was approved and the Town Meeting broke up with the singing of the 91st Psalm.

Zeke was one of those assigned to guard duty. Once a week he took his turn patrolling the river trail with his flintlock. But he saw nothing more alarming than a black bear and her big cub pawing the last of the wild grapes off the vines.

In the meantime word of John Oldham's murder reached Governor Winthrop, of the strong Massachusetts Bay Colony. The Governor decided that the Pequots must be punished. Believing that the people of the Connecticut settlements were too weak to do the punishing themselves, he sent his captain of musketeers swaggering down to Connecticut with the Boston Army to teach the Pequots a lesson.

"Did Captain Endicott fight the Pequots?" Zeke asked excitedly when Bejoyful told him this bit of news.

"It never came to a battle. He just marched into Pequot country and burned their villages. He went back to Boston without meeting a single Pequot warrior." Bejoyful was plainly disgusted. "All Endicott did was to make Sassacus madder than ever. He has set the whole Pequot tribe a-buzzing like a nest of poisonous hornets and now is safe in far-off Boston. We here in Connecticut will be the ones to be stung."

Fortunately for the Connecticut settlements, winter came early that year and there was plenty of snow. The Pequots were in a bad way because Endicott had destroyed so much of their food. Winter kept them too busy hunting meat to have time to attack the settlements.

When the snows melted, and the trails were clear, Bejoyful Elkins urged that forest patrols be started again. But the people of Wethersfield were no longer as worried about the Pequot danger as they had been in the fall. No one wanted to interrupt the activities of spring to prepare for a war that might never come.

Many new settlers arrived at Wethersfield that spring. The choicest bits of land in the vicinity were snapped up. Then greedy eyes were cast on the rich Wongunk lands along the river. People were heard to say that all Indians were treacherous, Wongunks as well as Pequots.

"It's dangerous to have those red heathen living so close to our village. Let's get rid of them before we are all murdered—like poor John Oldham."

At a town meeting someone urged that Sequin and his people should be forced to move away. Master Renfield stood up. His usually mild blue eyes were blazing with anger. His voice rang sharply through the Meeting House.

"Friends, we must not commit this heinous crime! The Wongunks have faithfully kept their promise of friendship to us. Sequin welcomed John Oldham and his companions when they first came here. Sequin sold them Pyquog. In return he asked only that he and his people be permitted to dwell near us always, that we protect them from the Pequots in case of war. You solemnly pledged him these things. In all decency, in all humanity, you cannot now, under God, go back on your word and drive our good neighbors away from the land that is theirs by every sacred right!"

One of the other settlers rudely bade Master Renfield sit down. "You talk like a scholar and a dreamer! Keep to your school teaching and let practical folk settle the affairs of the village! The Wongunks hold some of the best land along the river! We'd be fools to let these savages stay here while good English settlers are crying out for more land!"

Bejoyful Elkins heaved himself angrily off the bench. "If we must look at the matter from a purely practical point of view, we'd be fools indeed to drive the Wongunks away at this time. Hunting and fishing near the settlement; they are the best watchdogs possible to warn us of the approach of a Pequot war party."

The next day, however, some of the settlers went to the Wongunk village and told Sequin that he and his tribe must move away from the lands that their fathers had held from time immemorial. The English took their guns with them to back up their ultimatum in case the Wongunks refused to obey.

Sequin drew his blanket over his face to hide his sorrow. But he did not resist. He knew that there was no appeal from the decision of these flint-eyed white men with the fire-shooting sticks.

So the Wongunks scattered to find new hunting grounds.

The settlers betook themselves to their fields, with no thoughts beyond getting their crops into the ground.

And the trails around Wethersfield lay silent and lonely, except for the coming and going of the deer and other creatures of the wild.

CHAPTER 9
Raid

It was the fairest April day that Zeke had ever known. The buds on the maple trees swept the forest like a scarlet flame. The whistle of a quail sounded joyously across the greening meadow. Zeke whistled too as he drove Star through the field of flax. It was good to see the long furrows of rich earth turning back from the wedge of his plow. Good to know that Judith was over at the edge of the clearing digging dandelion greens for the dinner pot.

He turned his head to look at her. She had disappeared.

"Hi Judy!"

There was no answer; so she wasn't in the cabin either. She must have wandered into the woods again, to look for fawns, or to gather wildflowers. And after he had told her, and told her, that she must not go off by herself in these unsettled times!

Most people in and around Wethersfield had forgotten the Pequot threat, despite Bejoyful's warnings that danger would return with springtime.

He finished the furrow and turned Star loose, knowing that she would not stray away from the new grass. He caught up his musket and powder horn, and took a long, cold drink at the spring.

Judith was on the slope of a hill more than a mile south of the clearing. He found her picking yellow adderstongue, and had to smile to himself to see his formerly timorous cousin so unconcerned in the woods.

"I've always wanted to have a look at what's beyond that next ridge. Now that we've come this far, let's go on to the top."

She nodded, happy to follow.

They started off, Judith gamely trying to keep pace with Zeke's long, easy stride. He shortened his steps a little. On the climb up the steep side of the ridge he turned to give her a hand. Laughing and panting she scrambled up beside him. Small rocks that she had dislodged bounced and clattered down the ridge.

"If you want to be a good woodsman you'll have to learn to make less noise, Judy," Zeke told her. "Any Indian in the woods down there would spot us instantly by the sound of those stones. And try not to step on dry sticks. They go off like pistol shots."

"But there aren't any Indians in those woods," she protested. "We just came from there."

"Well, let's see what's on the other side—"

He led the way across the narrow ridge with its scrub oak growth and feathering of hemlocks.

They discovered that the rocky bluff on the other side fell

away into a dim and swampy tamarack wood. Through an opening in the trees they could see a faint trail threading its way southward. Zeke guessed that it was an ancient Wongunk trail.

Now that they had come this far, he longed to explore farther along that unknown path, but caution tugged at him. His eyes probed into the shadowy wilderness of the swamp, where spring green was weaving its delicate pattern in the tops of the ragged tamaracks.

"What do you seek?" Judith asked impatiently.

"Shh!"

Zeke felt rather silly because he didn't know himself what was troubling him. He jerked as he caught a flash of red brown moving swiftly through the swamp.

A big buck leaped into the trail and streaked along the base of the cliff. As he disappeared in the direction of Wethersfield his erect white tail flashed a danger signal.

"Now what frightened that buck?"

An Indian flitted like a shadow across the open bit of trail and vanished among the trees beyond. After him a long file of warriors moved silently up the trail.

Zeke's throat went dry. He grabbed Judith's arm and pulled her down flat in a thicket of hemlocks. "Look!" he whispered, nudging her.

A Pequot war party, no doubt of it.

Zeke could feel Judith trembling. He gripped her hand hard. He didn't blame her for being scared.

Some of the warriors were armed with rusty old matchlocks, but most of them carried bows and arrows. All had tomahawks and flint scalping-knives in their belts. Unaware of the eyes watching them, they trotted swiftly toward the settlement.

A few minutes later another lot went by.

Every tawny-red face was painted with streaks and splashes of brilliant color. Every head was plucked bald except for a narrow strip of hair running from the forehead to the nape of the neck. This scalp lock was stiffened with paint and grease until it stood erect. One or more eagle feathers were stuck through it.

"Zeke—"

Zeke could scarcely distinguish Judith's low voice from the murmur of the hemlocks about them.

"Zeke—are—you as s-scared as you were that time at the—cove?"

"No!" he whispered close against her ear. "They're only Pequots. I got away that time all right, didn't I?" He could see that she was trying hard to be brave, but her green eyes were wide with terror. "We'll be safe if we stay hidden—and don't make any noise. Uncle George is safe too. At this point they've already by-passed our clearing. But Judy, I've got to warn the village. And you must stay here."

"Oh, no!" She caught his arm with both hands. "Don't leave me alone, Zeke!"

"Shh! Listen, Judy, you are safe here. But you can't move quickly or silently through woods. I must go. If the folks in the village aren't warned in time they'll all be killed, Bejoyful and all the others. I wouldn't leave you if I didn't have to."

She bit her lips to stop their trembling. "Are you sure the s-savages won't come up here?"

"Not if you lie low and don't make a noise. Don't even breathe while you think there may be Pequots coming through that swamp. The main thing to remember is to stay quiet."

She nodded bleakly. "I'll be as still as a mouse."

He patted her shoulder and tried to smile into her tear-filled eyes. "Be brave, Judy. And remember—no noise—and stay hidden!"

"You be careful too, Zeke."

She gave him a white, strained look and then hid her face against the mat of hemlock needles.

Zeke crawled away, trailing his musket. He inched across the ridge top hugging the earth, wriggling on his belly like a snake. Every moment he expected to hear a Pequot arrow zinging up from the swamp. It seemed to take him hours to slither down over the farther edge of the ridge. But not a twig snapped, not a stone rolled under him.

When he was on the other slope he got to his feet and stole

down through the trees.

Now, with the hill between him and the Pequots, he could move fast!

The Pequots, in their plans for a surprise attack, were going around the long way behind the ridges. So Zeke had a good chance to beat them by making a beeline for the settlement.

As he ran he listened with dread for the sound of the Pequot war cry. But all was quiet in the forest ahead of him. The woods road led him into the midst of a peaceful scene along the river, where men and boys were at work in the fields. Women were trooping along the road from the village with baskets on their arms, carrying dinner to the workers.

"Pequots!" he shouted.

The word of fear flew downwind ahead of him.

People turned to stare at him as he tore along the road. Men snatched up the guns they always carried to the fields.

"Get back to the fort!" Zeke yelled. "Pequot war party—coming by—the—old—swamp—trail!"

The women picked up their skirts and ran. The boys and some of the men went with them. Others lingered to discuss the warning with their neighbors. A few continued stubbornly at their plowing.

By the time Zeke reached the village he was too breathless to do more than pound on cabin doors and gasp out the alarm. But others took up the cry.

"Indians! Indians!"

People scurried about frantically, rounding up live stock, fetching water in tubs from the spring. Some made for the little log fort; others stayed to defend their own cabins.

Bejoyful rushed out of his cabin, buckling on his sword while he roared out orders and herded folks indoors.

As Zeke turned back down the road a demoniac shriek quivered across the meadows. He dove for shelter behind a thick juniper bush.

Pequot war cry!

Plumed and painted warriors were swarming out of the woods. A whirr of arrows filled the air. Muskets exploded in the fields as the farmers shot at the oncoming Pequots. Their shouts mingled with the war whoops and screeching scalp yells.

One of the outlying cabins was already ablaze and warriors were pounding on the door with their hatchets.

Zeke took aim at a Pequot who had just tossed a burning candlewood torch on the roof of a cabin. Reloading hastily, Zeke blazed away at two warriors who were chasing a wounded settler. The shot hit one of them. The other spun around and hurled his tomahawk.

Zeke ducked and felt the air fan his ear as the tomahawk flew past. He worked furiously at reloading his musket.

Some older boys of the settlement now joined the fight with their long bows. Their marksmanship was as good as that of the

Pequots and their bows did more damage than the thundering blunderbusses of their fathers.

The raiders, however, were awed and confused by the sound and smoke of the matchlocks. Slowly they began to fall back across the meadows. Now, rather than sacrifice the lives of more warriors, the Chief in a shrill voice summoned his braves.

They moved so swiftly that they seemed to melt into the woods. Within a few minutes all of them had disappeared.

There was no sign of Indians in the forest, but Zeke did not relax his caution for an instant. Warily he crept up the side of the ridge—then at the last he could not restrain his eagerness. He raced to the clump of hemlocks where he had left Judith. He expected to see her run to meet him, but when he reached the covert it was deserted. There was no one but himself on the ridge!

Casting about feverishly in an attempt to find out what had happened to Judith, he found a large moccasin print in a soft patch of earth. Over near the bluff he found another. With a heavy heart he tried to piece together what had happened. He found where at least two Pequots had climbed the bluff from the swamp. But had they killed Judith or taken her away into captivity?

He slipped over the bluff and descended to the swamp. In the moist ferny trail he found the prints of many moccasins, going both ways. So the war party had passed here again on its retreat from Wethersfield!

With more searching he found the print of Judy's small moccasins among the others. He drew a deep breath and pushed his hair back from his wet forehead.

Judy had been alive when she reached this trail. Since they had not killed her at once, probably she was still alive. But what must be her terror! And alone. How he wished that he had let her take the chance of accompanying him to the village!

He shook his head to clear it of the tormenting thoughts. The thing to do now was to find Judy—and bring her back.

South along the trail, Judith's prints mingled with those of the hurrying warriors. These led him through swamp and deep forest to the bank of the river. Here, plain to read, were the marks where three big dugout canoes had been pulled up in the mud.

They were gone now. By this time they were well down the winding river on their way to the Sound. And poor Judy had been dragged along with them to the great Indian fort on the Pequot River.

CHAPTER 10

Uncas

Halfway home Zeke saw Uncle George and Bejoyful coming along the trail. It took only a glance to see that they were out looking for Judith. Her father had both his Scotch dag and the butcher knife in his belt, and his face was gray and drawn.

Telling Uncle George that Judith had been captured would take more courage than Zeke believed he had; he'd far rather face a hundred raging Pequots.

Bejoyful must have read the look on Zeke's face. "If there's anything you know, lad, be out with it."

"The Pequots had canoes down the river—" Zeke could not find the words.

"That they would. And—?" Bejoyful prompted gently.

Uncle George stepped forward, clasping Zeke's arm. "Ezekiel, my good boy, what is it?"

"I—I believe, sir, they've taken Judy with them."

Uncle George became paler, but he took a deep breath and thought a moment. "Tell us why you believe that, Ezekiel."

"Her footprints—" his voice broke, and for a moment the

three stood in unhappy silence. Then something about the way his uncle's clasp on his arm felt to him made him realize that he must have the hardihood to come straight out with it. "The small moccasin prints are together with theirs," he began. He recounted all that had happened from the time he had found her gathering flowers on the slope of the hill.

When Zeke finished his story, Master Renfield bowed his head and whispered, "God help my poor little maid."

"Amen," Bejoyful added, his head bowed too.

Zeke looked as if he were about to weep. He clenched his teeth.

Master Renfield noticed it. "Do not chide yourself, Ezekiel, for having left her there, hidden, so you could the better hasten and warn the village. You acted wisely."

"Aye," Master Elkins added, "for there's no knowing how many lives you saved, and a brave fine lass she was to stay alone and let you go."

"Something untoward must have happened to discover her to the Pequots," the schoolmaster reasoned.

"Uncle George, there's only one thing to do. I'm going after her."

Both men shook their heads.

"It is bad enough your uncle has his daughter to worry for," Bejoyful said. "You can only add to his anxiety by being away too."

"Gid Ash will look after matters for Uncle George the few days I'll be away," Zeke said. "I'm going to ask Nemox to help me find Judy."

"Ah," Bejoyful nodded, "that is likely. Trust a Mohegan to know the secret trails.

"I will accompany you," Master Renfield said. "Let us make preparations at once."

Zeke and Bejoyful looked at him in dismay.

"Master Renfield," Bejoyful began, "no lone Englishman could hope to approach that Pequot Fort, and two would only increase the difficulty. The Mohegan boy could, however, get into it. But Zeke must reach him as soon as possible."

Before many more words were spoken, Master Renfield saw the force of the trader's tactful argument. "Aye, I'm no woodsman, Master Elkins. My presence would only slow up the expedition, and every hour is precious if my child is to be rescued."

"No time will be lost, friends," Bejoyful said, taking them by the arm and leading them homeward. "Here is my plan. I am ready for my spring trading trip to Mohegan Town. They'll be expecting me there. Now, Zeke will come along with me. He'll be a help, and so I'll say he's my helper." Bejoyful's big eye winked, as if he could cheer the two Renfields now. "Whilst I dicker with the oldsters, Zeke will be making arrangements with Nemox."

Within an hour Zeke was getting ready. He always kept his

weapons in good condition, but now he whetted his knife and hatchet to a biting keenness. He worked even harder cleaning and greasing his musket, renewing the flint with care. Then he melted a bar of lead in a heavy dipper. He poured the lead into a bullet mold which had closing handles like a pair of scissors so that he was able to work quickly and soon turn out enough bullets to cram his pouch full.

He then took a few hours of sleep. He got up quietly so as not to waken his uncle, and went down into the root cellar where he felt around in the dark for the keg of gunpowder. Filling two powder horns, he picked up his provisions and stole out into the dark to meet Bejoyful at the village landing by dawn.

All day they traveled through deep forest. Bejoyful's two pack horses were heavily laden with goods which he expected to trade for furs at Mohegan Town.

"Mohegans are a small tribe but a rich and thriving one," he told Zeke, "and the reason for it is that Uncas is cunning and burning with ambition to become the most powerful Sachem in this entire Connecticut valley. So he drives his folk to prosper."

To make an impression on Uncas, the trader had attired himself in his finest doublet and breeches. They were of green velvet, and he wore scarlet hose with them. His sword was slung in a baldric of tooled Cordovan leather studded with silver.

Zeke felt shabby in his patched breeches and an old buff coat which was too short for him and getting tight across the shoulders. But it mattered little to him. All he could think of was finding Judy.

Just before twilight they came out on the shore of a clear little lake, surrounded by gardens and cornfields. At the far end, a stockade crowned a gentle hill. It was Mohegan Town.

Near the path that led to the stockade gate, boys were playing football. Zeke scanned them eagerly to pick out Nemox, but the friend was not there.

A tall brave stood at the gate.

"Koue!" the trader called.

"Welcome, Elder Brother," the Mohegan said in his own tongue as he passed them in. "It is well your packs are large. Old Warrior Winter left a bountiful harvest of fur in my traps last year."

When the eyes turned upon Zeke, they continued to shine as though he was dressed as gloriously as Bejoyful, but the admiration was obviously for the flintlock. Zeke smiled back. He wouldn't have traded his gun for all that Bejoyful wore or carried.

As soon as they were in the village, children came thronging noisily after Bejoyful, and followed him as he drove his packhorses across the square. He certainly was a popular person here, Zeke could see. Warriors lounging before their lodges shouted boisterous greetings to him, and the squaws cooking supper at the outdoor fireplaces waved and called "Koue!"

Bejoyful pulled out a pouch of sugar suckets and caraway cakes for the children surrounding him. "Here, my hearties, a sweet for each of you!"

Zeke stared with lively curiosity at the comfortable arched-roofed lodges made of saplings and bark. Fronting on the square were the Council House, the Sachem's lodge, and the Guest House.

This last one was where they were to stay, Bejoyful told Zeke.

Nowhere, however, was there any sign of Nemox.

"Shall I ask somebody, Bejoyful, which house he lives in?"

"No, if Nemox isn't here by now to welcome you, it is either that he is out hunting or that he has some good reason of his own for not coming right out. Anyhow it's not well to ask questions of folk here. Just bide your time and appear happy to be among them."

At the Guest House, it seemed as though every squaw in the tribe wanted the visitors to taste her cooking. More and more gifts of food kept arriving in maple burl bowls and dishes of birch bark and clay.

They sat down to a supper of baked beaver's tail, roasted cattail potatoes, and a salad of watercress and the young fiddleheads of ferns. Their dessert was roasted green pinecones flavored with sugar. The tea was made of the tender young twigs of black birch, spiced with checkerberries.

Zeke wondered whether Judith was getting anything as good as this to eat among the Pequots. A tight feeling gripped his chest whenever he thought of his small cousin in their hands.

After supper Bejoyful took Zeke with him to call on the

Sachem, bringing him a green cloak bedizened with gilt, some huge beads of glass, a pewter bow, and a chunk of pink coral.

Uncas received the guests at a small fire in his lodge.

He was the most impressive man Zeke had ever seen; haw-featured, lean and hard, big enough to dwarf his tallest warrior. His black eyes had a gleam that cut right through you. Zeke had to pluck up a bit of extra courage to meet that dark glance firmly.

The Sachem seemed well pleased with the gifts, and offered Elkins the Calumet. Zeke expected Nemox to come in and join them any moment. It was good to think that this great man was the uncle of one's good friend, but the friend did not appear, and Zeke became anxious.

As they were about to take their leave, Uncas said gravely in Algonquin, "Brothers, we are happy to have you here. But bear well in mind that my cloak covers also any others who come while you are here." His eyes stabbed at them across the fire.

Afterwards, on their way back to the Guest House, Bejoyful turned a worried look toward Zeke. "It seems that he's expecting other visitors, people that he thinks we might not get along with. Another trader, perhaps."

"Do you suppose it may have anything to do with Nemox not being here?" Zeke wondered.

"I don't know," the trader answered. "I thought I knew these people well, but this is new to me, and seems strange."

CHAPTER 11

Watch the Red Belt!

After Bejoyful finished his bargaining with the Mohegans next morning, Zeke helped him to cord the bales of fur.

Outside, the stillness was broken by excited voices and the sound of many feet.

"The other guests must have arrived," Bejoyful said. He swept aside the woven grass door-curtain to look out. "God save us," he whispered softly back to Zeke. "They're Pequots!"

Across the square stood six Pequot warriors, magnificent with plumes and paint. Mohegan Sagamores, in quilled robes and wearing eagle feathers in their roached hair, were ceremoniously welcoming them. After a deal of stately palavering they all stalked into the Council House.

"Pequots are here to no good," Bejoyful said.

"From what Nemox once told me," Zeke replied, "I think they're going to try to get Uncas to join them on the warpath against us Owanuxes. Oh, I hope Nemox shows up soon!"

Some boisterous young braves trooped into the square and started to plant a post between the Council House and the Sachem's Lodge. It was smeared with paint and decorated with a tuft of feathers.

"That's a war post." Bejoyful's usually jolly face wore a gloomy look. "Appears there'll be big doings here tonight. If the Pequots persuade Uncas to take up the hatchet and strike it into that post, it will mean war."

A feeling of trapped helplessness swept over Zeke. Here were Bejoyful and he alone in a village of Indians who at any moment now might turn upon them as enemies.

Some older warriors were looking with stern disapproval toward the noisy group around the post.

"Young braves long for war so they can win their eagle plumes," Bejoyful explained. "They don't care much who the enemy is, whites or Indians like themselves."

At twilight, musicians seated in front of the Council House began to tap softly on drums.

Uncas came out of his lodge, attended by a train of plumed Sagamores, the lesser chiefs of the tribe. Over his shoulders was flung a mantle made entirely of the feathers of scarlet tanagers. It shimmered in the light until he appeared to be wrapped in flames.

He entered the Council House, followed by the Mohegan Sagamores and Wise Men.

The square was thronged with Mohegans. The fragrance of ceremonial cedar-wood fire drifted in the evening air. Everybody was listening intently to the highflown oratory going on in the Council House between Uncas and the Pequots. Zeke and Bejoyful, seated discreetly inside the door of the Guest Lodge, so as not to appear inquisitive, tried to listen also. But at the distance they could not make out the words.

"The fate of all New England may depend on the sounds we are now listening to," Bejoyful said.

The door curtain moved slightly as though a breeze had pushed it. An Indian wearing a deerskin cape stepped in. "Koue, Brother."

"Nemox!"

"We must speak low," Nemox said. "Much to tell. But first you, Zeke, tell me. Why you come here? I know why trader come. But why you?"

Zeke started to answer in Algonquin.

"No, speak English. If Mohegan outside here, he not understand."

Zeke told how the Pequots had attacked Wethersfield and captured Judith.

When he had finished, Nemox said in a low voice. "Brothers, I saw little girl."

"Where?"

"When?"

Nemox stepped back and sat down on one of the fur bales. Zeke and Bejoyful drew close to him in the dim room.

"Brothers, the Fisher hunts alone. I hunt many birds for Sachem. Bring him beautiful feather. My brother fisher-cat help me. Also I bring Sachem news of Owanux and Pequot. Two days ago I see Pequot canoes, little Owanux girl in one."

"Did you know she was my cousin?"

"No. I follow them down river long way. This afternoon get back to Mohegan Town. My aunt say you here. Pequot here too. My aunt say don't tell anybody Owanux boy your friend; maybe anybody tell Pequot. So I wait for dark."

"What about your uncle the Sachem?" Bejoyful asked.

"He your friend."

"But he's friendly with the Pequots too."

"Yes, Uncas keep Pequot friend too. He not know yet which way to jump, Owanux or Pequot. Over in Council House, Pequot bring him present. Big, fine red war belt. Uncas look but not put on. Maybe he send back to Sassacus. Maybe not."

The voices from the Council House swelled to a hideous pitch.

"What if Uncas doesn't take the belt?" Zeke asked.

"Pequot fox wait," Nemox said, then chuckled. "Belt very beautiful."

"Nemox, will the Pequots hurt my cousin?"

"Maybe, maybe not. Maybe they hold her for hostage. But together we find her, bring her home."

"You won't be able to help Zeke find her if your uncle throws in with the Pequots," Bejoyful said. "Do you think he might do so?"

"I don't know, Elder Brother." Nemox answered while the din of voices rose outside. "Pequots kill Wongunk and Uncas say he sorry. Owanux at Wethersfield take land from Wongunk, Uncas very angry...Hear that? They talk about Wongunk at Council House now.

Both Bejoyful and Zeke then told Nemox how the Renfields and the Ash family, and other settlers had tried to prevent their greedy neighbors from taking the Wongunk land.

"Yes," Nemox nodded. "Bad Owanux and good Owanux."

Outside, all had grown quiet. Soon drums began beating loudly.

Nemox got up. "Big dance ready. Big dance for our guests. You guests, Pequot guests. You go watch. Maybe war dance too. Hope maybe not."

He slipped away.

Zeke knew that it was imperative that no one in Mohegan Town see him and Nemox together. There were many war-eager young bucks who might become suspicious.

"Our best hope," Bejoyful said, "is that Nemox will tell his uncle in time that many of us at Wethersfield didn't want to chase the Wongunks off their own land. It might influence the Sachem in our favor."

"Whatever happens, I'm going to the Pequot fort."

"Aye, Zeke," Bejoyful murmured. "I guess you have it in you to do just that."

Lean, broad-shouldered Zeke had been toughened by hard work with ax and plow so that he looked as strong as a grown man.

A blending of willow whistles and the thin piping of reed flutes mingled with the sound of shell rattles and the throbbing of drums.

Bejoyful and Zeke stepped outside into darkness where showers of sparks were swirling skyward from a huge fire in the center of the square. Through the flames they could see the war post with a gleam of scarlet around it like a great snake.

"That's the Pequot war belt," Bejoyful said. "It will hang there until Uncas accepts it, or until he kicks it around the post and sends it back to Sassacus. That's what to pray for."

Young warriors, with arms held chest high and hands dropped like paws, began to circle the fire in the shambling gait of the Bear Walk. Some wore bearskins with jaws agape and teeth gleaming above their dark faces.

Swaying and shuffling, they circled the fire. Around and around, shuffle, shuffle, heel and toe, to the beat of the drums, the wailing of flutes like wind in the pine tops, the weird, swishing music of tortoise shell rattles.

Around and around, faster and faster, leaping and whirling.

There was the Medicine Man in a grotesque cornhusk mask. There was Nemox stripped to breechcloth and moccasins, leaping high and prancing. The Indians watching were shuffling their feet and clapping their hands to the quickened tempo of the music.

Zeke thought of Judy, alone and terrified in the Pequot camp where they'd be having frenzied barbarous dances like this almost every day.

The dance was changing. Now it was more like a war dance than the Bear Walk. Nemox dropped out, but he did not come near Zeke.

Braves, their faces streaked with black and red paint, shook their tomahawks on high, or stooped low to earth, as if they were stalking an enemy. A hurled hatchet struck the war post below the flashing red belt.

"Ho, ho, ho!" shouted the young warriors.

"Wah, wah!" roared the elders in disapproval.

Uncas was watching from in front of the Council House. Suddenly the music died, the dancing ceased, deep silence fell as everyone turned to stare at the crested Sachem. The firelight played on his giant form and proud, stern face. Before him a path opened to the war post with its garland of sinister red wampum.

A warrior ran up and offered his tomahawk to the Sachem. "Smite the post, Oh War Chief!"

Uncas fingered the tomahawk and looked at the post. In the vibrant silence the dreadful moment of his indecision seemed to stretch out until Zeke thought that it would last forever. If the Sachem's tomahawk struck the war post it would rouse the whole Mohegan tribe to war against the English! Zeke's mouth went dry. He pictured burning cabins, friends killed or captured, perhaps he and Bejoyful killed before they could leave this town. And poor Judy—

Uncas dropped the tomahawk and turned away from the war post.

Drawing his feathered cloak across his face, he strode to his own lodge and went within. For a moment the people looked after him in silence. Then the drums began to sound again and the dancers to prance and whirl. But now it was no longer a war dance.

Uncas had not struck the post. The tomahawk lay unused, there on the ground before it. But high on the post the red belt of war still hung in evil splendor, showing that Uncas was still undecided.

And as long as it would hang there, Zeke and Bejoyful knew, it meant a constant threat to every English person in the Connecticut Valley.

When the two got back to the Guest House they hoped to find Nemox waiting for them. He was not there. Nor did he come later.

CHAPTER 12
Pequot Country

At sunup Zeke rolled his few belongings in a blanket. As a last thought he stuffed his pockets with cakes of ground maize and honey left from breakfast. A fellow going secretly through the forest and not daring to fire a gun could live a long time on such food.

As Bejoyful and Zeke drove the fur-laden horses across the dancing place they saw the great belt of red wampum still on the war post. It seemed now to wink a sinister farewell to them. Uncas had not decided to wear it, but might do so yet!

Nobody else in the village was astir this early after the long feast of roast puppy dogs last night. At the stockade gate, the guard who passed them through wore a sullen look. In answer to it Bejoyful pushed his hat far back on his head and drew in great breaths of sweet morning air.

But the truth was that neither he nor Zeke was feeling easy about Nemox's not having come sometime during the night to arrange for going to the Pequot fort. Their only hope was that since they had to leave Mohegan Town this morning anyhow, Nemox was probably figuring that the best way to join them unobserved would be to meet them somewhere out on the trail.

As their way wound deeper into the forest, Zeke watched anxiously for sight of him. "Probably his uncle won't let him go. Then what?"

Bejoyful looked somber. "Then we'll have to do what we might have in the first place had you not thought to go with Nemox: wait for English forces to storm the Pequot fort. If you went there alone, you'd only be one more captive. You and Judith could never escape unaided."

"I must go there despite that," Zeke answered. He became more and more frightened at the very thought of it. He remembered Bejoyful once saying he too was afraid sometimes but had to keep on going—saying it to Judy, in fact. "I can't abide the thought of her in that place all alone." Zeke added.

A few feet ahead of them a dark face with a pleased grin rose slowly from some ferns behind a fallen tree. "It has been a long wait," Nemox said in Algonquin.

Fringed deerskin shirt and leggings, a turkey feather slanting jauntily in his loose hair, a pack roll made of a fur sleeping-robe—he seemed quite ready for the trip. As he glanced down and saw the pouch he had given Zeke, he touched the long knife at his own belt happily. "Brothers, I have much to tell you."

The three sat down on the log while the horses nibbled at some tender grass.

Nemox's reason for meeting them on the trail was the same as they had expected. He had left the village long before daylight so that nobody would see him.

"I could not come to see you last night, because there was not a moment when somebody's eyes were not on me. Did you see Uncas leave the hatchet lying on the ground?"

"Yes," Zeke replied in Algonquin. "Do you think, Nemox, that your uncle will finally accept the war belt?"

"He does not yet know any better than you, Brothers, or I, whether he will or not. After he went into the Council House, I saw him and he told me that as he stood there holding the hatchet he could feel both the sky and the earth telling him to wait for a sign. Then I told him how the good English tried to prevent the bad English from stealing the Wongunk land. 'That is my sign,' Uncas said. 'Now I will not join the Pequots in war until Hobomoko says I must.' So he is sending me to Matchit-Moodus to our Grandmother Ninigret. There I will await the message from Hobomoko for Uncas."

"You can't then help me rescue my cousin?" Zeke's hopes crashed.

His friend's dark face broke into a mischievous smile, and whispered in English, "Uncas say maybe Hobomoko take long time. We give him plenty time, Zeke, what?"

Bejoyful slapped his knee and roared, "Nemox my boy, I hope someday you become Chief of all the tribes in North America!"

Nemox shook his head. "Wah! Better is it to be friend than Chief. Uncas not happy. Nemox happy." He stood up and swept a half a circle with his arm. "We travel around Pequot country. Come at fort from north. Only lone hunter go that way. Zeke and Nemox one lone hunter."

In a few more moments Bejoyful took his leave. When the green curtain of the firs closed around him, and Zeke could no longer see Bejoyful or hear the hearty voice again in conversation, he felt cut off from all that was safe in the world.

There was no trail that he could see, but Nemox seemed to know exactly where he was heading. After a few moments of silent walking, Zeke became aware also of the reassuring weight of the flintlock on his arm. His friend carried a bow and a quiver of the finest arrows over his left shoulder.

Several days later they came out on the upper waters of a river that flowed between pine covered hills.

"Pequot River," said Nemox. "We swim. Pequot fort downstream on other side."

Searching along the bank for a log on which to float their packs across the river, they found an old canoe half submerged in the foam and litter between some rocks.

"The spring floods must have washed it down from some winter camp," Zeke guessed. He dragged it out on the bank. There was a large hole in the birch bark side, but the sturdy cedar frame was still intact. "If we patch it, and hide it handy to the fort, it will do to ferry Judy across the river. She can't swim."

Nemox squatted down beside the canoe and poked it here and there with his finger. "We patch," he said, standing up. "But first we find shelter. We hide before Pequot hunters find us."

Zeke swam the river, pushing a log on which his gun, Nemox's bow, their packs and clothes had been lashed with vines. Nemox pushed the water-logged canoe. On the other bank Nemox dumped the water out of the light craft and swung it onto his shoulders. Zeke carried both packs.

They started cautiously downstream, keeping as close to the river as possible. Although their moccasins left little trace, Zeke took every precaution to cover their trail. And he kept looking for a birch tree from which he could peel bark for a patch. He found one growing in a copse of smaller trees, and cut his strip of bark low down on the trunk where the scar would not show.

Nemox meanwhile looked around for a place where they could hole up. When Zeke returned to where he had left the packs, Nemox led him to a cave-like recess beneath an overhanging ledge of rock, high on the river bank. Thick scrub hemlock screened it from the river. It was a perfect hiding place, even large enough for them to have the canoe inside.

Now that they were deep in Pequot country they dared not risk a fire, but they carried cooked venison in their packs.

In the morning Zeke stayed in camp to patch the canoe. Nemox, familiar with the territory, scouted the Pequot fort, which was about a mile down the river.

Zeke did not leave the shelter all day except to fetch in some spruce roots for sewing on the canoe patch. He chose a young tree and dug up the fine, threadlike roots. After he cut out as many roots as he thought he needed, he carefully swept the dirt back with his fingers, then sifted leaves and pine needles over the place until he was satisfied that all signs of his work had been covered.

Later he looked for fallen branches that could be shaped into canoe paddles. With no tools he could do only the crudest sort of job patching the canoe. He used the point of his knife for an awl. A fishhook helped to poke the spruce roots through the holes he made. For a really watertight patch he needed to apply a coating of melted pitch pine, but even without it, this patch would hold long enough to get them across the river.

Toward sunset Nemox slipped through the hemlocks.

"Did you see her?" Zeke asked eagerly.

"Judy at fort," Nemox said, squatting down apposite him. "I hid on ledge above spring. White girl came to fetch water. I parted ferns that hid me. I said your name. Then Pequot girl came. I hid again."

Zeke let out a great breath of relief. "Is she all right?"

"She seem good," Nemox replied. "Later I crept close to village. Judy sat with old squaw outside stockade. They chew buckskin to soften it. I think old one is seamstress, Judy her helper."

"Tomorrow I'll go with you," Zeke said, fingering his sheath knife nervously. "We'll get her away from there."

"Wah. It more safe for me to go alone. I hide by spring.

When Judy come we make plan for her to meet us at night in forest."

CHAPTER 13

One Against Many

Zeke was alone when he awoke the next morning. It was a day of sticky, breathless Maytime heat. The air under the rock ledge was heavy with the scent of the surrounding evergreens. A swarm of black flies invaded the shelter and crawled into his ears and down inside his shirt. They bit and bit until he thought he'd go crazy.

Through the hemlocks he could see a sparkle of light where the hazy sun shone upon the river. If he but dared go for a short swim! It was the only way to get rid of these pesky flies.

His shirt was soaked with sweat. The red lumps on his skin burned feverishly. He began to feel a little light-headed.

He left the musket behind and crept along the ledge, taking care not to crush the ferns growing in the crevices, then stole down through the trees to the water. The voice of the river was the only sound.

With eager fingers he stripped off his sodden shirt and washed it in a deep pool, spreading it on a rock to dry. He took off his other clothes and slipped into the water. Its coolness flowed over him. He dove like a muskrat and came up shaking water from his hair and eyes.

Flies ceased to bother him. He swam about and then floated on his back, marking the high flight of an osprey downstream toward the sea.

He came up out of the water and pulled on breeches and moccasins, then reached for his shirt. Just as he yanked it over his head, something grabbed him.

Flailing his arms and kicking out frantically in an effort to free himself from the hands that clutched him, Zeke struggled to get his head out of his shirt. He was thrown to the ground and held down while his hands were jerked back and tied with a length of rawhide. Then someone seized him by the hair and dragged his head up out of the shirt.

He saw a fierce copper-colored face glaring down at him. Still gasping for breath, he looked around. He was surrounded by Pequots!

"Owanux!" A Pequot spat out contemptuously.

Another Indian gave Zeke a vicious prod with the toe of his moccasin. Zeke took the hint and stood up.

The oldest Pequot fingered a flint knife and stared pitilessly at Zeke. "What do you in Pequot country?"

Zeke shrugged as if he did not understand.

"Wequesh!" the old one called, and in answer to that name a thick-set warrior stepped close to Zeke.

He had the cold eyes of a copperhead. "How came you here, Owanux?" he asked in English.

"I'm a hunter. I lost my way and have been wandering for days."

"Where gun?"

"I lost it." Zeke gnawed his lip and held himself very tight to keep from trembling.

Two of the Pequots began to range over the river bank and through the woods, looking for his tracks and his gun. Rigid with dread he waited for the yells of triumph that would announce the discovery of the shelter. What if they lay in wait there and capture Nemox too! Oh, why hadn't he let the flies chew him up!

The hunters returned empty-handed.

Zeke breathed more freely. He had hidden his trail well.

They started downstream to the Pequot fort. Wequesh herded Zeke ahead of him, prodding him with his tomahawk every few steps.

The fort was a stockade village much larger than Mohegan Town.

Pequots came rushing from fields and lodges to see the Owanux prisoner. Whooping, yelling, jostling, they surged about him. Women pinched him and threw gravel in his face. Children thrust sticks between his legs to trip him.

With a sick feeling, Zeke thought of Judy. Would they also treat a girl captive like this? He glanced about, hoping to see her. But there was only the sea of ferocious dark faces, ugly with hate. His step faltered and Wequesh hit him a hard clip with a tomahawk.

Zeke forced himself to endure it all without a cry or moan. His lot would only be harder if they guessed that he was afraid.

But his nerve almost failed him when he saw men and boys forming in two lines. They were armed with sticks, switches, and clubs. He swallowed hard as he saw Wequesh fingering a club spiked with thorns. They grinned at Zeke maliciously: they'd make him run the gauntlet.

Someone cut loose his hands and pushed him forward. At the end of the double row of Pequots he could see the red war post. If he could reach that post he knew he'd be safe from any more blows, but the chances were that they would knock him senseless before he could get there.

He crouched down to get a good start. With an ear-splitting yell he shot forward.

The Pequots were whooping and dancing. They kept getting in one another's way as they tried to land their blows on Zeke. Whack! Thump! Whack! He dodged and zigzagged down the line, shielding his head with his arms. Seeing a break in the line, he charged through it.

There was a momentary confusion among them, and he ran on free for a short distance. He leaped over a stick that a boy slyly pushed in front of him. A dozen pairs of hands shoved him back into the lane. The blows began to fall again, harder.

Just ahead he saw Wequesh. The husky Pequot was grinning

as he hefted his thorny club.

Half crazy from pain, Zeke lowered his head in fury and butted Wequesh in the stomach with all his might.

Wequesh let out a howl and dropped his club to clutch at his stomach.

The others roared with laughter. But this didn't prevent them from trying to hit Zeke as he sped on past them.

He was nearing the end now. He staggered and almost fell as an extra hard blow struck him. Blood drummed in his ears. But he must not stop—he must not fall! He waved his arms to keep off the clubs. He twisted and feinted to avoid one Indian—drove his fist into the face of another.

Then he was out of the lane, lunging for the war post with his last ounce of strength. His whole body throbbed with pain as his two hands found the rough wood and clung there.

The shouts of the Pequots sounded faint and far. Weak and dizzy, Zeke leaned his forehead against the post.

A squaw pushed him toward a nearby lodge. He staggered inside and fell down on a bed of furs. That was the last he remembered.

CHAPTER 14
Yellow Jackets

When Zeke awoke it was dark in the lodge. Through the doorway he could see the reflection of a fire. He turned over. Every inch of his body was aching.

A little squaw entered the lodge and thrust a clay pipkin of hot broth at him. "You drink!"

The herb-flavored broth made him sleepy.

The next time he awoke it was morning. He got stiffly to his feet, feeling stronger, but he was still one big ache.

The squaw appeared in the doorway and beckoned him outside where her family was gathered around a large clay kettle of steaming chowder. They were all dipping into the common pot with clamshell spoons. And among them was Wequesh! Neither he nor any of the others looked up to notice their captive guest.

A girl of about Judy's age handed a clamshell over her shoulder to the squaw, calling her "Yotash."

Zeke glanced around, wondering where in this town Judy might be.

Yotash gave him the shell spoon and pushed him into the

breakfast circle.

Zeke hesitated when he saw the children searching with their dirty fingers for the chunks of lobster meat that floated in the chowder.

Yotash shoved Zeke between Wequesh and a young girl. Wequesh grunted, moved over, and continued his breakfast.

Half-heartedly Zeke dipped his spoon into the pot. After a while, Wequesh finished his breakfast and stood up. "Oh-guh-oh," he grunted, patting his stomach as a compliment to the cook. He motioned Zeke to his feet. "You come! See Sassacus."

As Zeke limped through the town he felt the full effects of the beating he had taken. A lump above one temple made his head throb. Ugly bruises on arms and shoulders showed through his tattered shirt.

The Pequots stared and jabbered.

Wequesh marched him to where the Sachem was enjoying the spring sunshine outside the stockade. Zeke steeled himself to meet the piercing glance unflinchingly.

"You know how make gunpowder?" Sassacus demanded.

Zeke knew the Pequots were in need of powder, for lack of which their few muskets were useless in the war against the English. If they believed he would help them make some gunpowder they might spare his life.

He nodded wisely.

"You show Pequots?"

Zeke shrugged. "I would need—"

"What you need?" Sassacus asked impatiently.

"Some moose fat, for one thing." Zeke thought he was safe in saying this, because Nemox had told him that the moose had wandered north this year. Mohegan hunters had not shot one.

"We get moose fat." Sassacus' face hardened to a cruel mask. "You fool us, Owanux, and you die!"

Zeke followed Wequesh back past the lodges outside the stockade and kept glancing about in hope of seeing Judith. He stared at every small girl, but did it covertly so that Wequesh wouldn't suspect he was looking for her.

"Koue, Kaw-Kout," Wequesh said politely as he came opposite the lodge nearest the spring.

An old squaw grunted a reply. She and a girl were scrubbing a pegged-out doeskin with a smelly mixture of deer's brains and water.

Zeke's eyes slid past the girl and then jerked back as he realized that the tumbled mass of her hair was of a chestnut color. His heart jumped. Judy? But no! Not that skinny little thing in the tattered deerskin tunic!

He looked again. Now he was sure it was Judy! He saw Wequesh's eyes going shrewdly from her to him. So he looked back and forth from her to Wequesh.

"Is this an English girl?" Zeke asked as innocently as he could.

At that, Judith turned around. There was a start of surprise in the green eyes peering furtively from the tangle of her hair.

Zeke knew his bruised and swollen face took on the look of a stranger. "Who are you, little girl?"

"I-I'm Judith Renfield of Wethersfield," she said. "Who are you, poor boy?"

"Jack O'Lantern."

Judy bit her lip and made a face that puzzled both of their captors.

Wequesh grunted and strode on.

Zeke had to follow. He held back his sigh of relief. Thanks to Judy's quick little head, no Pequot knew yet that he was here to help her escape.

All the way to Yotash's lodge, though, he kept grieving over little Judy. She looked so scrawny and overworked.

If he could only get in touch with Nemox. But after the way he'd messed things up, he feared Nemox had probably gone back to Mohegan Town in disgust.

Several times Zeke had to accompany the squaws and young people to the forest to gather firewood. Judy also went along on these occasions, but Zeke was watched so closely that they had no chance to speak.

Once, she paused near him and pretended to be adjusting the bundle of faggots on her back. Her voice reached him in a thin whisper. "Did—did the savages harm my father?"

"He's safe," Zeke murmured without looking at her and heard her deep-drawn breath of relief. "Uncle George wanted to come with us."

Judy paused a moment and then said very carefully, "Listen, Zeke. When Nemox comes to the spring he signals me with the song of a thrush."

Kaw-Kout called to her, and she hurried away.

Zeke went with Yotash next day to fetch water from the spring. Yotash stopped at Kaw-Kout's lodge and Zeke was left outside with the bark buckets of water. He edged over to where Judy sat cross-legged beneath a tree, sewing porcupine quills on a doeskin shirt.

Some Pequots were sauntering past. Zeke watched his cousin in silence, marveling at the way her little fingers worked and tugged at the tough sinew thread, and went painstakingly about the business of anchoring each prickly, slippery porcupine quill.

She used a flint awl to punch holes in the leather. Her needle was of bone. From time to time she would glance at a piece of birch bark on which Kaw-Kout had drawn a design for her to follow. In little clay dishes around her were barbless quills. They were dyed with colors—red, yellow, green—mixed from plants and berries.

Zeke put down his buckets and squatted beside the piece

of bark, as if he were admiring the design. Judith gave him a quick smile and bent over her work again. Her low voice barely reached him. "I saw Nemox this morning. He will be waiting to guide us to the canoe the next time we go wood-gathering."

"If they watch me too closely you must go alone."

"No!" Her eyes were lit by a flash of courage. "We'll go together. We'll find a way."

Zeke stood up. A lump rose in his throat as he looked at his small, valiant cousin. "Judy, is Kaw-Kout cruel to you?"

She did not lift her eyes from her sewing. "At first I cried all the while and she would throw cold water on me or beat me with a willow switch. Now I am quiet and do as she bids."

"The old weasel!"

"But the worst of all was when they told me that they had burned Wethersfield and killed every settler." Judith dropped her work to dig her grimy little paws into her eyes. "Oh Zeke, I never expected to see you or my father again."

When next they went to the forest Zeke stayed as close to Judith as possible. The "thrush" was singing by the river. Zeke worked in that direction, heaping up faggots as if he intended to collect them on the way back.

Not far from him, Judith was stuffing pine cones into a sack.

Slowly they drew away from the others.

Judith slipped out of sight around a thicket of laurel.

Zeke walked aimlessly a step or two. Before him some yellow jackets were swarming around a hole in the ground where they had a nest.

Yotash called to him, beckoning. Behind her Kaw-Kout came hurrying.

"Eagle!" Zeke yelled, pointing upward and then made as if to run toward it.

They glanced up but followed him directly.

He tore away.

Yotash started after him and blundered into the yellow jackets' nest, crushing it with her foot. The maddened wasps poured out.

"Ee-yow!" She capered about, slapping herself as if she had gone crazy. She turned and ran frantically back through the woods, Kaw-Kout stumbling blindly at her heels and a cloud of yellow jackets following them.

Soon the forest resounded with the tortured cries of Pequots who hopped and danced with pain as they swatted one another with hemlock branches trying to drive away the furious little yellow warriors with their fiery stings.

In the confusion no one missed the Owanuxes.

Zeke and Judith made for the river.

A lithe brown figure shot out of a thicket to race ahead of them.

When Zeke and Judith were dashing down the river bank Nemox was already knee deep in the water, steadying the little canoe. Zeke's musket was lying in the bottom of the boat, together with the rest of their scant equipment.

Judith tumbled into the canoe and settled herself amidships. Zeke knelt in the bow and took the paddle. Nemox took his place in the stern. The canoe floated away from the bank and drifted downstream in the green shadow of the trees.

Nemox guided the canoe diagonally across the river. They came to shore just above the bend. While Zeke and Judith gathered up the equipment, Nemox piled stones in the canoe and shoved it back into the river, where it sank.

CHAPTER 15

The Big Boulder

At Twilight, Nemox called a halt on a knoll from where he could watch their back trail. "We rest till moonrise."

Zeke unrolled his blanket and made Judith lie down. "After I left you that day on the ridge, what happened so that the Pequots found you?"

Judy put out her hand and patted his arm. "It wasn't your fault, Zeke. I just didn't wait long enough to make sure that the Indians had gone by. And when I started to crawl back to our side of the ridge I must have made a deal of noise. Anyhow, all of a sudden there were two big Indians coming after me."

He was sorry now to have reminded her of that dreadful time. Yet it was a relief to know that all would have been well if she had stayed hidden.

"And you did find me," she finished, wiping away her tears with the sleeve of her sleazy old deerskin tunic.

"Yes, and we'll be back home in no time," he promised rashly. "Try to sleep a little now."

Zeke sat down beside Nemox in the shadow of a big rock. This was a good time to draw the old charge in his musket, to set a new flint, and to reload.

An hour later radiance filled the sky as the moon climbed above the pointed tips of the dark pines.

Nemox stood up. "Wake Judy."

They drank from a spring that trickled down the side of the knoll. Nemox then led the way through mile after mile of silent, moon-dappled forest. The going was easy in this open, park like woods. Judy made a gallant effort to match the pace of the two boys.

At last, Nemox said, "We stop till morning."

They splashed through the waters of a brook and made their camp on the other bank under a huge hemlock whose feathery branches swept the ground, forming a tent-like space behind them.

From his pouch Nemox took the last three cakes of meal and a chunk of maple sugar, which he broke into three pieces. As soon as Judith had eaten her last crumb, she fell asleep. The boys lay down on Nemox's robe with their weapons beside them.

Zeke awoke in the gray, breathless dawn. Nemox was crouched near him. The air was filled with a low mutter of thunder on the hills westward.

"Sounds like a bad storm," Zeke said, sitting up.

"Hobomoko!" Nemox spoke through stiff lips.

With Zeke close behind, he crept to the edge of the bank. Thick white mist hung over the brook. Moisture dripped from the firs all around them as they lay watching and listening.

The mist lifted slightly.

Zeke felt Nemox touch his arm. Nemox was staring up into the branches of the pine that towered next to their hemlock. Following his gaze, Zeke made out an animal stretched along a high limb, like a big cat taking its ease on a fireside settle. Gleaming devil-eyes looked down at the boys with lazy curiosity from a furry, pointed face. Zeke recoiled instinctively. The fisher-cat had probably been watching them for hours.

But Nemox was pleased to see his totem. Quietly he raised one arm in salutation.

The Nemox in the tree bared his long teeth in a snarl. Then suddenly he was on his feet. His short legs flashed noiselessly along the branch. A whisk of his bushy tail, like black smoke in the swirling mist, and he vanished into a hole in the trunk of the pine.

Both boys immediately flattened out on the bank. What had disturbed the fisher?

Their eyes ranged warily, upstream and down.

Zeke stiffened as he saw a Pequot step out of the forest upstream and wade across the brook. Four more followed, moving as silently as ghosts. Not until they had disappeared among the trees did the boys dare to move.

"Nemox warned us," the Mohegan nodded. "Now we move fast, before Pequots strike our trail!"

Zeke woke Judith, warning her in a whisper.

Following Nemox, the cousins slipped over the bank and stole downstream. When the bank became too low to hide them, Nemox took to the woods at a swinging lope.

Zeke kept glancing back. After they had gone several miles toward the hills, and even stopped once to rest, his roving eyes picked out shadowy figures on their trail down the dim aisle of the forest.

"Pequots!" His voice crackled with excitement.

Nemox stopped for a look.

"I see five!" Judith cried. Her fingers clutched Zeke's tattered sleeve.

"And four more!" Zeke added.

Nemox faced the hills again. "Follow," he said over his shoulder as he started for the long ridge toward which they had been heading all morning. Zeke pushed Judith ahead of him. "Run!"

A burst of speed carried them to the base of the ridge. Its side was much too steep to climb. But Nemox streaked toward a ravine that cut into the steep side, and Zeke followed with Judith. They waded a brawling brook and dashed on, knee deep in ferns. Behind them the yells of the Pequots sounded terrifyingly near.

The ravine opened up before them. It was steep and narrow, with big trees finding footholds here and there. It seemed to point the only way up to the top of the ridge.

Zeke looked back. The Pequots had gained on them and were coming like tireless hounds on a hot blood scent. The burly warrior in the lead was Wequesh!

Zeke's chest felt tight, for a moment it was difficult to breathe. Swallowing hard, he sprinted after Judith.

"Run, Judy! Run!"

"I—I can't go any faster!"

He clamped his free hand around her wrist and pulled her along.

They went scrambling up over great rocks, slippery with moss, dripping with ferns.

An arrow whizzed past Zeke's ear and struck a rock ahead of them. Zeke whipped behind a big boulder and jerked Judith down beside him.

A bowstring twanged from the shelter of a tree trunk just above them as Nemox returned the Pequot's shot.

Wham! A Pequot arrow drove deep into Nemox's tree.

Zeke took careful aim with his musket. Bang! The shot echoed and re-echoed along the cliffs.

A screech from the Pequots: someone had been hit. They dove for cover, dragging the wounded man with them.

Bang! Zeke fired at the last Pequot in sight and saw the eagle plume fall from his scalp lock.

Judith peered around the edge of the rock but ducked back in a hurry as a flight of arrows sped toward them.

Nemox answered with two in quick succession.

"Keep down!" Zeke told Judith. To Nemox he called softly. "Can you see them from up there?"

"One." Nemox let fly with another arrow. "One no more," he grunted.

"How many arrows have you left?"

The Fisher-Cat rashly thrust out an arm with five fingers wide apart. A bow twanged below and an arrow blazed his arm before he could draw it back.

"Zooks! Don't take such chances! Are you hurt badly?"

"A scratch," Nemox said calmly.

"Save those arrows in case they rush us. You'll have to stand them off while I reload."

That was their greatest danger, an attempt by the Pequots to rush their position. This would probably have been done before now if the Indians had not been disconcerted by the unexpected firing of the musket.

Zeke glanced to where Judith was collecting a pile of good-sized rocks.

"These are my bullets," she said.

She started to lean back against the big boulder, and then jerked away. "Be careful, Zeke. This rock is wobbly."

"So it is." Absently he set it rocking with his hand. "I hope it stays here while we need it for a fort."

He dropped down and crawled to the edge for a glance down the ravine. There was not a Pequot in sight.

"They're hatching mischief down there," he muttered.

Something like a thick brown snake slid up through a bed of ferns between two boulders.

Zeke's gun flashed up. A shot rang out.

"Eee-yow!"

The other Pequots came climbing up the ravine.

Zing! Zing!

Nemox shot twice and ducked behind his tree as a shower of arrows sped toward him. Zeke's musket banged again. Then Nemox shot a third arrow.

Some of the Pequots had been hit, but there were several left in the narrow ravine, and they were getting nearer and nearer.

Zeke fired again. Nemox shot his last two arrows while Zeke was reloading.

Then Judith began to hurl her rock ammunition at the enemy.

A Pequot was scrambling up a ledge just below them. Judith threw her biggest rock and hit him squarely between the eyes. He toppled backward with a howl. The rock went clattering down the ravine, carrying a landside with it.

Zeke stared at the slide. "Zooks! That's it!"

He laid down his musket and pushed with both hands at the big boulder. It rocked forward and then settled back.

Nemox slid down the slope and ranged himself beside Zeke, shoving hard. The boulder stirred—rolled back.

"Again!" Zeke grunted

Together they strained at the rock. Judith got next to Zeke and pushed with all her might. Slowly the great boulder moved out of its bed. Little by little they turned it toward the brink. All at once it plunged, almost carrying Nemox with it. Zeke grabbed his friend's leather shirt and dug his heels into the hillside. Judy clung to a little cedar tree with one hand, to Zeke with the other.

With a roar the huge rock bounded down the ravine, carrying hundreds of other rocks along with it leaping and rushing upon the startled Pequots. They stumbled and slid in a mad scramble to get out of the way but were caught between the walls of the ravine.

"Climb!" Nemox shouted at his companions.

The rest of the way up the ridge became so steep that Judith was using both fingers and toes. In the worst places Zeke boosted while Nemox pulled her from above.

Panting, they found themselves up against the sky. At last they dared stop to look back.

The big boulder had come to rest against a larger rock at the bottom of the ravine. Piled up around it were rocks, earth, and small trees it had harried down in its slide.

The Pequots had retreated into the woods below.

Nemox waved his arm toward the other side of the ridge. "Down there—Matchit-Moodus!"

No Pequot dared pursue them into the home wood of Ninigret the Wise Woman. From the ridge top they could see the blue Connecticut sparkling between forest clothed hills on its way to the sea.

"There's our own river," Zeke cried. "Zooks, it's almost like being home just to see it again!"

Nemox smiled. "We go down to river. Come, Judy. Come, Zook."

Judith laughed as she followed down the gradual slope. Zeke laughed too. It was their first merriment in a long time.

CHAPTER 16

Hobomoko Speaks

They reached a brushy ledge. Judith caught Zeke's arm. "Look!" she cried in a tight voice.

A panther, stretched out lazily on a high rock, was watching them with his golden eyes.

Zeke pushed Judith behind him.

"Koue, Loks!" Nemox called.

The great, tawny cat rose with slow grace.

"Does he know him?" Judith whispered.

The panther jumped down and padded over to rub against Nemox.

"Lead us to Ninigret, Younger Brother," Nemox said confidently.

Zeke watched nervously the huge paws with their sheathed claws.

Loks turned his sleek head to stare at Zeke and Judith. Gravely he walked over to sniff at them.

Zeke braced himself. Behind him, Judith caught her breath

sharply.

"Been stealing any turkeys lately, Loks?" Zeke asked in as friendly a voice as he could manage.

Loks ignored him and fixed his glinting eyes on Judith. To Zeke's amazement Judith put out a timid hand and touched the panther's velvety head.

"You're a beauty," she said, a little breathless. Her fingers scratched softly at the base of his ears. Lok's eyes closed to shiny slits. He rubbed against her and his purr rumbled deep in his chest. She gave Zeke a happy smile. "He's not very different from Tabby Paws—only bigger."

When they continued on their way, Loks padded beside Judith and she kept her hand on his muscular neck.

The ledge shelved down to a forest of spire-like pines.

Out of the violet dusk of this wood, appeared a tall Indian woman. She carried a staff in one hand. On her back was a bundle of wood herbs.

Loks bounded forward to roll at her feet like a kitten.

Nemox stopped, with Zeke and Judy peering wide-eyed over his shoulders.

"Welcome, Nemox."

She was very old, yet as straight as a sapling birch. Her wrinkled face had the same eagle cast as those of Uncas and Nemox. Her dark eyes were lit by strange fires.

Nemox, speaking in Algonquin, told the Wise Woman about their escape from the Pequots.

Ninigret beckoned Zeke and Judith closer. "Welcome, children of the Owanux," she said in a low, grave tone, and then took her way along the hillside with Loks pacing beside her.

The three young people followed.

Ahead of them, deep in the shadow of the pines, the dark entrance to a cave showed among the rocks. A cold breath blew from it, a breath from secret places deep within the earth. A waiting silence hung there.

"The cave of Hobomoko," Nemox said softly.

Judith walked close to Zeke, and Zeke himself felt uneasy. Perhaps it was because the shadows lay so deep and still about this cave, perhaps because Nemox was so plainly awed by it.

Ninigret led them along the hillside to another cave. It was shallow and had a floor of clean white sand spread with fur robes. A fire burned in a stone fireplace before it. Nearby was a clear, icy spring. Juniper and sweet fern perfumed the air.

They drank at the spring and washed their grimy faces and hands. Judy combed her hair with her fingers and tied it with a bit of ground cedar. Zeke pinned up the rents in his breeches with wood splinters.

Loks wandered off to hunt his supper.

Nemox and Ninigret talked near the fire. He told her the story of the Pequot visit to Mohegan Town.

Her face became stern. "Uncas may not approve, Grandson, that you were so unwise as to take the roundabout way instead of waiting here at Moodus for Hobomoko to speak."

Nemox did not flinch before her darkling glance. "My brother Zeke needed my help," he said simply.

She nodded. "Friendship has its dues. Yet you did wrong. You must tell the Sachem this."

"I will tell him," Nemox agreed.

If the god had spoken while Nemox was not there to carry the message to Mohegan Town, the wrath of Uncas would indeed be hard to face.

"How long since the Terrible One has spoken?"

"Not for two moons. But certain signs tell me he will speak soon."

"Grandmother," Nemox asked anxiously, "will Uncas go on the warpath against the Owanux? Must my brother Zeke and I fight as enemies?"

Ninigret's eyes had a faraway look. "Uncas must choose one side or the other in this war."

"But which, Grandmother?"

"The Sachem's heart does not lean to either side. His heart cares only that Mohegans remain free people."

She walked away through the deepening twilight, to light the ceremonial fire at Hobomoko's cave.

Zeke and Judith joined Nemox at the fire, where Ninigret had left venison steaks broiling on sharpened sticks over the coals. Cakes of crushed strawberries, mixed with honey and cattail root flour were baking on hot stones. Judith served supper on clean slabs of bark.

While they were eating, an oppressive stillness crept over the hillside. Clouds rolled up over the ridge to hide the stars. The fire flickered. Shadows closed in dense and black.

Nemox looked upward and then gave Zeke a meaningful nod. A thunderstorm was surely forming.

Judith was so sleepy from the hard day they had been through that she did not notice this. Soon she went into the guest cave, and Zeke helped her arrange a pile of sleeping robes at the back of it.

When he came out again, Nemox met him and said, "Judy very brave. Had plenty scare today. But if Hobomoko speak tonight, maybe too much scare for Judy. Good she sleep."

He and Zeke went over to a bed of ferns and sat down. They could see both caves from here, though the night seemed darker than ever. Silence hung like a dead weight on the air.

Near the entrance to Hobomoko's cave a tiny fire lit the blackness beneath the great pines, like a star at the bottom of a well at midnight. Ninigret was crouched over the fire, inhaling the fragrance of black birch and aromatic herbs while she muttered charms. Loks was beside her, his head resting on his broad paws, his brooding eyes reflecting a gleam of firelight.

"If Hobomoko comes," Zeke whispered to Nemox, "do you think we'll see him?"

Nemox shook his head, "See, no. But hear. Hear him across the river."

"Can Ninigret see him?"

"I not ask Ninigret that," Nemox answered. "So I not know. I know sometime Hobomoko speak from inside cave. Sometimes from up sky. Big time from both together. Then big message. Maybe big war."

Even while Nemox was talking, their ears caught a mutter of thunder in the sky. Or did it come from the sky? It might have rumbled from the depths of the mountain for all they could tell.

Again the thunder came. Now it rolled. The earth trembled. It was slight but certain. Nemox and Zeke sat up straight and looked at each other a second, and then at the black-mouthed cave.

Another tremor. Loks crept closer to the Wise Woman. Zeke could see in the firelight the panther's sleek sides heaving.

The earth shook. Loks raised his head and cut the night with a tearing scream.

A mighty wind tossed the pines. Weird crackling noises exploded from the mouth of the cave and at the same time the earth seemed to shudder.

Ninigret rose to her feet and faced the dark entrance. Loks, still close beside her, stood a little in advance. Together they disappeared into the cave.

A crack of thunder followed and came back in a deep sounding echo. Great rocks seemed to be rolling about inside the earth.

Nemox slightly clenched his fists, maybe fearing for Ninigret, Zeke thought, as he himself feared for her now.

The wind died down. Everything everywhere became still. Soberly Ninigret emerged with her panther from the cave.

Nemox stood up. "Hobomoko has spoken," he whispered reverently. His grandmother beckoned, and he left Zeke.

Zeke went to the guest cave to look in on Judy. She slumbered soundly. He stole outside again.

Nemox was gone. Above the pines the clouds were rolling away. Stars were winking out. It was as if there had never been any noises at all.

CHAPTER 17
Down the River

At dawn Zeke saw Ninigret and Nemox walking away from the other cave. The Wise Woman was talking earnestly. Nemox was listening with a solemn expression. They passed out of sight among the trees.

Later, Ninigret returned alone. Nemox had started for Mohegan Town with Hobomoko's message, she told Zeke, but her face wore a calm, closed look that seemed to forbid any questions concerning Hobomoko and his affairs.

Quietly she set about preparing breakfast. Judith helped her, while Zeke collected firewood.

Judith asked the Wise Woman timidly if she and Zeke would be staying long at Moodus.

"You go today," was Ninigret's surprising answer.

"You mean we're going home to Wethersfield?" Zeke asked eagerly.

"Wah! You must go down river, Nephew. War is bad upriver, bad downriver too. But going down will help you if Pequots come in big war canoes."

Zeke nodded. It was true that paddling alone, he could not

hope to beat a war canoe in a race upstream. Down at Saybrook he and Judy could take passage home on some large boat.

"You start tonight, reach Saybrook at dawn," Ninigret said.

"Nemox left no message for me?" Zeke ventured.

"Wah."

"Then it must be that Hobomoko advised the Mohegans to go to war against us English." Zeke said heavily, "Nemox didn't say good-by, because we are to be enemies."

Ninigret closed her eyes and thought for a moment. "You will know some time," she said.

After telling Zeke and Judy to rest for the long trip ahead of them, the Wise Woman went away on some business of her own. But Loks stayed near them all day, helping Judy to forget her anxiety as they tussled and romped together.

At moonrise Ninigret returned. She and Loks led Zeke and Judy down the mountain, past a village of bark wigwams where Medicine Men were holding dances in honor of Hobomoko. A number of birch canoes were drawn up on the river bank near the village.

Ninigret pointed to a small one. "There is your boat, my children. Stay clear of both banks. Land only at Saybrook fort."

They tried to thank her. A smile glimmered across the Wise Woman's face, like starlight on dark water. "Go with strong hearts."

Judith patted Loks' head. Then she seated herself in the canoe. Zeke pushed off and knelt in the stern.

His paddle dipped and flashed. They shot out into the broad, strong-flowing Connecticut.

Looking back as they turned south, they saw the figures of Ninigret and Loks in silhouette against the flames and the blowing sparks of the powwow fire. Snatches of chanting floated over the water. Then the canoe swept around a bend and they found themselves drifting in a lonely world of charcoal forest and moon-silvered river.

Zeke's work with the paddle consisted mostly of steering. The strong current swept them along. But there were snags to look out for, and the dread that every cove they passed might hide Pequots waiting to attack travelers. And mixed in with that dread was the dark thought that he may have lost his best friend, Nemox, because of Hobomoko's words.

Judith dozed and awakened again to find the black wilderness still slipping past on both sides. "It seems like we've been going down this river forever," she said in a hushed tone.

The sun came up in an opal sky. The river was widening out. Zeke strained his eyes ahead in hopes of seeing Saybrook fort. Bejoyful had once told him that it stood on a peninsula on the west bank.

"Zeke!" Judith cried suddenly. "There's something moving on the bank. It's Indians! Oh Zeke!"

He turned his head and peered toward shore. The light was

stronger now, making it easy to see the Indians under the trees. They were putting a big dugout into the water!

"They're taking after us!"

"Sit still!" Zeke said through tight lips.

The canoe drove forward as he put every ounce of his strength behind the paddle.

But in the dugout twelve paddles flashed in unison. The big boat plowed through the water. Distance between the two boats lessened. Zeke leaned on his paddled and did not look back.

Judith clenched her hands in her lap. There was no extra paddle she could use.

The pale light of early morning now showed green tidal meadows ahead, spired with dark cedar trees. The smell of salt marshes sharpened the air. Seagulls wheeled above the vast reaches of the river, mewing harshly.

"I see the fort!" With a gasp of relief, Zeke steered the canoe toward the sturdy earthwork that jutted out into the river.

The lookout at the fort sighted both canoes. The sun glittered on armor as other men climbed up beside him. Seeing white people in the leading canoe, they shouted encouragement. A couple of them ran to man the swivel gun on the wall. A shot rang across the water.

Several Pequots dropped their paddles and took aim with their bows.

"Zeke! The Pequots are going to shoot us!" Judy yelled.

"Get down as low as possible."

A flight of arrows whizzed toward them. One of them struck Zeke in the arm. An explosion of pain ran up to his shoulder. Every movement sent a new wave of pain through him, yet he dared not stop paddling to pull the arrow out.

The dugout was only a few lengths behind now.

Judith tried to rise to her knees in the speeding canoe.

"Stop that!" Zeke shouted.

"I'll pull that arrow out of your arm."

"Sit still or you'll upset the canoe!" Desperately he wondered whether his wounded arm would hold out until they reached the fort.

Boom!

The round shot whirled past them and struck the high prow of the dugout, shattering the tip. The Pequots backed water frantically.

Zeke kept on with dogged strokes of the paddle.

Now that the Pequots had lost the race, they turned and plowed across the wide river. The canon boomed again and a shot hurtled after them. But it only churned up the water harmlessly as the long canoe disappeared behind an island near the east bank.

Zeke was dizzy with pain as he guided the canoe to the wharf below the earthwork. Men ran down to help them land. One lifted Judy out of the canoe. Zeke got up and stepped ashore.

Strong hands took hold of Zeke while someone grasped the arrow close to the head and snapped the shaft.

"The head will have to be cut out," said a deep voice. "I'll take him to the Great Hall. Dame Gardiner will look after him."

CHAPTER 18
Flaming Arrows

Zeke's wound kept him in bed a whole week. Dame Gardiner and Judith nursed him tenderly.

The Gardiner house stood midway on the peninsula between the river fort and the log stockade that protected Saybrook from the mainland. Almost every day the salt breezes carried sounds of banging guns and Indian war whoops to Zeke's room. Lieutenant Gardiner told him that the Pequots had been besieging Saybrook for months. No one could go outside the stockade to fetch in firewood or work in the fields, except under strong guard. Even then they never got back without a fight.

Gardiner had only twenty-four men to fight the hundreds of Pequots who lurked near the fort. At Cornfield Point, across the cove, he had built a blockhouse to prevent the Indians from burning the corn which must feed the settlers through the winter.

"The Indians hope to starve us out; they may succeed if help does not come soon. Most of our cattle have been killed. Ammunition is running low."

Pequots in big war canoes controlled the river. They boarded all boats trying to go up or down and killed or tortured the crews. Now the settlers were afraid to venture on the river at all. It was weeks since any word of the upriver colonies had reached Saybrook.

Zeke stirred uneasily in the big, curtained bed.

Wethersfield could be burned to the ground, Uncle George and Bejoyful killed or captured! And if his parents had started for Wethersfield this summer, as they had planned, they might have been attacked by a Pequot war party!

"And the Mohegans too may be on the warpath by this time," the Lieutenant said. Deep lines of worry tightened around his mouth. "I'd give a round sum in gold to know what message your Wise Woman sent to Uncas."

Zeke's arm was still sore but the inflammation was gone. Dame Gardiner told him that he could get up the next day.

In the morning, when he poked his head eagerly between the bed curtains, he saw that his filthy, tattered clothes had disappeared. On a stool beside the bed was a pair of frieze breeches, a linen shirt, hose, shoes, and a buff jerkin. A wooden tub stood on the hearth with a kettle of hot water beside it. There were towels and a jar of bayberry soap. Zeke jumped out of bed and padded over to the tub.

Half an hour later he went down to the kitchen, dressed in clean clothes and feeling like a new boy.

Dame Gardiner greeted him cheerily. Judith was rocking a wooden cradle near the open door. She gave a cry of joy when she saw Zeke. She was such a different Judy from the forlorn girl of the Pequot fort! Her skin shone, her hair glittered with cleanliness. In a linen gown and a starched apron, she looked as neat as a buttercup.

"Look, Zeke." She caught his good arm and pulled him over to the cradle. "The Pequots wouldn't let me touch a papoose, but Dame Gardiner lets me mind David. I have to be careful because he's very new. It could be he's the first Owanux baby born in Connecticut!"

Judith set a place at the table and fetched Zeke a bowl of soup and a flagon of milk. Then she brought a pewter dish heaped with golden brown fried cakes, crisp and spicy-sweet. "I helped Dame Gardiner make these. They're krullers—Dutch cakes."

Lieutenant Gardiner came into the kitchen wearing a steel corselet and helmet. A sword hung by his side and he had a brace of pistols in his belt. "There's gunfire at Cornfield Point," he said. "The Pequots must be attacking the blockhouse. I'm going over there with some extra ammunition for my men."

Zeke stood up. "I'll go with you, sir."

Gardiner looked dubious. "Are you fit?"

Both Dame Gardiner and Judith protested that Zeke was too weak to leave the house. But Zeke wasn't going to stay around there with the womenfolk while other fellows did the fighting. His flintlock stood in the chimney corner. The powder horn and bullet pouch hung from a peg near the door. He slung them on and followed his host out of the house.

A shallop lay at the wharf under the guns of the river fort.

Zeke went on board with the Lieutenant and three others. The sail was run up and the boat started across the cove to Cornfield Point.

As they approached the Point the men on the shallop could see smoke and flame spurting from loopholes in the blockhouse walls. Not a Pequot was in sight, but fire arrows were cometing toward the blockhouse roof from the long grass edging the cornfield. Several arrows lodged deep in the tinder-dry slabs. Tongues of flame licked at the roof.

One of the defenders crawled out to throw a bucket of water on the flames. An arrow sent him crashing to the ground. The fire spread rapidly.

On the boat Lieutenant Gardiner rapped out his orders. "Charles, Hugh, and I will hold the neck of land with swords while the men in the blockhouse run for the boat. Peter and Zeke will back us with their guns."

Zeke was nervous and tried to hide the fact by pretending to check his musket. He guessed that a fellow never did get used to this Indian fighting. He looked up and met Peter's honest eyes. Peter was as uneasy as he! Somehow that helped to steady his hands.

As the shallop nosed the wharf the men in the blockhouse gave a cheer. From the cornfield the Pequots raised their screechy war cries.

Gardiner sprang ashore holding a pistol in one hand, his sword in the other. With Charles and Hugh close at his heels, he ran toward the cornfield. Pequots rose out of the grass and swarmed out of the woods.

Zeke and Peter took positions near the burning blockhouse and began firing as fast as they could.

Arrows zoomed at them like brilliantly colored dragonflies. Muskets exploded. Pistols barked. Thrown tomahawks rattled against the breastplates of the three swordsmen.

A dozen Pequots surged between Lieutenant Gardiner and his comrades. Gardiner's sword was like a half circle of light as he held the squawling warriors at bay. He lunged with the long blade, driving them back.

A bowstring twanged and an arrow pierced his thigh. He staggered. The Pequots closed in on him.

Manfully Hugh and Charles struggled to cut their way through the throng of savages to their leader.

Zeke and Peter moved up closer, firing turn and turn about. As Zeke was ramming a charge into his musket he heard Peter shout. A whole mess of warriors were dragging the brawny fellow away toward the woods! Zeke ran after them and shot his gun into the group. The Pequots scattered, then came back to engulf him like a wave.

His gun was gone. He was on his back, kicking and struggling. A big warrior, painted like a rattlesnake, lunged at him with a tomahawk. Zeke rolled away and came to his feet, still fighting.

Back in the forest a war cry quivered in the air like the howl of a hunting wolf. A chorus of savage voices echoed the sound. Then a splendid chief came leaping across the cornfield with a pack of warriors ranging at his heels.

"Uncas!" Zeke shouted.

Painted for war, his red hatchet flashing, the Sachem of the Mohegans was coming to the aid of the English at Saybrook.

"Ho Zeke!" rang a familiar voice.

Zeke found himself fighting shoulder to shoulder with Nemox, who was proudly wearing his first war paint.

Everywhere the Pequots were falling back before the fierce attack of the Mohegans. They retreated into the forest. Soon the noise of battle died in the distance. Zeke did not follow beyond the edge of the trees and Nemox turned back with him. The Fisher-Cat's quiver was empty and Zeke's bullet pouch almost so.

Lieutenant Gardiner was helped on board the shallop by those of his men who had survived the fight. "Well, Zeke," he said, "now we know what advice your Mohegan friend carried to Uncas from the Wise Woman of Moodus."

Uncas with his victorious warriors strode down to the wharf and went on board the shallop. The sun glistened on the tossing eagle plumes in his scalp lock. Outlined in black upon his broad chest was the totem of the royal Wolf Clan. He met Gardiner's searching glance with shrewd, twinkly black eyes. "Pequots gone from here," he said simply. "Return no more. We go now to Pequot fort. Make end of them."

"The people of Connecticut will never forget how you helped them," said Gardiner.

"Ha-oh!" the Sachem grunted. "Mohegans and English, brothers forever." He took the Lieutenant's hand and pumped it up and down, almost crushing it in his enthusiasm.

CHAPTER 19

Upstream

Now that the river was safe, Lieutenant Gardiner agreed that the young Renfields could go home. Nemox persuaded Uncas to let him take his friends upriver. He chose one of the smaller Elmwood dugouts for the journey. Uncas sent two Mohegan braves to help Zeke and Nemox paddle the canoe.

They started early in the morning, after a grateful farewell to Lieutenant and Dame Gardiner.

As they drove against the current opposite Matchit-Moodus, all three Mohegans stopped paddling a moment to waft pinches of tobacco toward the shore. Zeke and Judy looked eagerly for some sign of Ninigret and Loks. But the great trees on the mountain hid the cave. And the village by the river seemed only a collection of deserted wigwams.

Halfway home they sighted white sails billowing against the green hills that bordered the river. Three ships were bearing down upon them. The decks were crowded with men, many in armor.

As the vessels came opposite the canoe, Zeke saw a big man waving to him from the rail of one of them. A hearty voice boomed over the water. "Ho Zeke! Ho Judy!"

Zeke and Nemox lifted their paddles. Judith snatched off her apron and waved it over her head.

It was like being home again just to see Bejoyful's ruddy, smiling face.

Nemox steered the canoe closer to the ship.

"What fleet is that?" Zeke shouted.

"We're the Army of the United Colonies of Connecticut," came the proud reply. "We're on our way to the Pequot fort. We're going to end this war!"

The ships were drifting rapidly past on their way downstream. Zeke cupped his hand to his mouth so that his voice would carry. "Be-joy-ful! Did my—folks—come—out to—Wethersfield?"

Bejoyful shouted something but the wind caught his words and tossed them to the hills. Zeke thought he heard the word "Indians." He called again, anxiously. Bejoyful shook his head to show that he could not hear. He waved his hat in farewell as the fleet left the canoe behind.

Zeke, in the bow of the canoe, was the first to sight their own fields, a moment later the cabin with its chimney-smoke curling lazily against the blue summer sky.

"Our pocconock!" Judy waved both her hands to the lush meadow. Zeke could see the cornfield well now. The corn had grown high and green. Gid must have finished the planting.

The Mohegans brought the canoe to shore at the foot of the

meadow. With his flintlock in his hand, Zeke leaped up on the bank. He reached his free hand to Judy. She landed lightly beside him and together they tore away through the long grass to their cabin.

Nemox and the two warriors followed in more dignified fashion.

Someone came out of the cabin.

"There's Uncle George!" Zeke shouted. He waved excitedly.

And that strapping fellow with the ax couldn't be anyone but his brother, Roger! "Roger!" he yelled. "Hi Roger!"

Roger raised a shout. Uncle George lifted his hands, and then both hurried down the slope to meet Judith.

Zeke's father and mother and Hope popped out of the cabin. Alan came striding from the barn. Tabby Paws jumped out of the green covert of Judith's mint bed.

All the Renfields were there to welcome the wanderers home.

They set upon him and Judy with happiness that was quite at odds with their usual reserve. They wrung his hand, clapped him on the back, hugged him and kissed him with an enthusiasm that may have seemed little short of lunatic to the three watchful Mohegans.

Zeke longed to look around, to see how things had gone during his absence, but first he and Judith had to tell their whole story.

Zeke's mother acted as if Judy and he hadn't had a thing to eat in all the time they had been away. She and Hope set out a feast on a long table beneath the trees.

When the shadows of the elm trees began to lengthen across the clearing, Nemox rose from his place at the table beside Zeke. "We go now. We join Uncas at Pequot fort." An eager, proud look came into his dark face.

Zeke stood up too. "You will win your eagle plume in this war, Nemox."

"Ha-oh! We win good peace for all in this war! Owanux will work their fields, Indians hunt in woods. No more will Pequot war cry wake the dawn."

Zeke and Judith walked back to the canoe with their friend. After all they had gone through together, after losing Nemox, and then finding him again, it was hard to say good-bye.

"Remember what my father told you," said Judith. "This is your home too now, Nemox. Wherever you go we'll always be waiting for you to come back here."

Zeke couldn't picture a future without Nemox. "We've plans for running a trap line up a hidden valley this winter."

"I come, Zook! I come soon." Nemox smiled. He grasped Zeke's hand warmly, and then stepped into the canoe where the two plumed warriors sat waiting for their young Sagamore.

The Fisher-Cat picked up his paddle; before he dipped it in the water he raised it in farewell to the two friends on the bank. "Netops, Zeke. Netops, Judy."

"I'll be watching for you, Nemox," Zeke called through cupped hands as the canoe shot down the river.

THE END